GOD'S FRONT PORCH

Gerald Eugene Nathan Stone

TATTERSALL
PUBLISHING

Tattersall Publishing
P.O. Box 308194
Denton, Texas 76203-8194

www.tattersallpub.com

Printed in the United States of America

00 99 98 97   010   1 2 3 4 5

Cover: Drawing by Rob Milton
        Photography by Jonathan Reynolds

Library of Congress Catalog Card Number: 97-60455

ISBN 0-9640513-9-7

Stone, Gerald Eugene Nathan (1929-   )
God's front porch / Gerald E. N. Stone
     Summary: Snakes, tornadoes, and river baptisms are among the many trials
and tribulations faced by a young, disaster-prone Baptist preacher in rural Arkansas, humorously related by a sympathetic parishioner.
     [1. Clergy - Fiction. 2. Baptist Church - Clergy - Fiction. 3. Arkansas - Fiction.]

ACKNOWLEDGEMENTS

My older brother, Ladru, became a published author in his teens—some pulp magazine in the 1930s. I have treasured that short story through the years, but it also has intimidated me, as I looked to him to become the writer in the family. After sixty years, I got tired of waiting, so with his encouragement I have begun.

Even so, I would not have made it to this point but for the encouragement of my editor, Crystal Wood, who is a writer in her own right. She and her cadre of helpers have massaged this manuscript so long that I can see her fingerprints on every page. Any déjà vu that you experience must fall to my account—her editing scissors succumbed to overuse.

To my wife, Virginia

*The weaving between the woof of illusion
and the weft of reality is the fabric of a story.*

*This little book with its characters, incidents, and places
is very real . . . somewhere . . . I suppose.*

*Don't let the struggle to separate the two
lessen your joy of making their acquaintance.*

1

PREACHERLESS AGAIN

We'd run through the last three preachers pretty fast. Like Buford, who lived on his pig farm up on the ridge overlooking Blacksburg (and one of the few Methodists around here) said, "Hit don't make no difference—pigs or Baptist churches. When either one gets the scours, it gets kind of messy."

Most preachers leave a church because the Lord has called them elsewhere. I understand that in the business world the expression they use is "tender their resignation," but that may be just a face-saving way of not getting fired, so you can get hired somewheres else. At Blacksburg Baptist Church, we cut through that mustard. We didn't ask for a resignation, we didn't have a going-away pounding, and we didn't hug everybody when we got rid of a preacher—we fired him. Like Millard Doss said, "Pray that your firing may not be in wintertime nor on the Sabbath, but pray that you've got some friends or family to take you in." That may be in the Bible.

Our last preacher hadn't run off with anyone's wife, or skimmed the offering plate. Those reasons are pretty common elsewhere, but not here. We didn't pay enough to make running off feasible, nor was there anyone here worth running off with. As for skimming, a preacher would have done better to hunt for arrowheads in the Bend and sell them at Fort Smith during the annual rodeo, or steal newspapers and tin cans from the Boy Scouts.

We fired that last preacher for using the Revised Standard Version in his annual Associational sermon over at Ola in October. It was not only heretical, but plumb embarrassing to our church. You see, we'd always been the weak sister in our Association. The other churches poked fun at us because we'd never won an Attendance Banner. And then that preacher of ours had to go and smear egg on his face and ours, using that infidel version to preach from. I will agree that Brother Adler, our oldest deacon, shouldn't have tottered down to the front at invitation time the Sunday after the Association meeting and spit on the preacher.

But the preacher made a mistake at that point, and I don't sympathize with him none for what happened next. He stood there in shock, and then had the audacity to open his Bible and read about "blessing them who despitefully use you"—all the time using that same Revised Standard Version. After that, the other deacons got up and went down the aisle, and one by one, they knelt in brief prayer before they followed Brother Adler's lead and got up and spit in the preacher's face. Needless to say, we lost several families after that, but we also purged ourselves of that modernistic leaven.

Our Associational Missionary, Brother Eben Dothan, came the Sunday after we showed the preacher the front door, and tried to oil down the waters, and at the same time to prod us into electing a pulpit committee.

I opened my big mouth about all the dissension we'd been having, and what did it get me? That's right—stuck on the pulpit committee. One thing about Baptists, we sure know how to reward loose mouth.

Like when Buford made that remark about Baptists. He didn't expect it would come back to haunt him, but the next day, when he stopped the school bus to pick up a handful of kids on the highway (he drove the bus for Lamar High School, where the Blacksburg kids go), there was Annie Koontz, president of the Woman's Missionary Union at the church, waiting for him with the kids at the bus stop. She had her arms akimbo, bonnet off, and legs spread apart. He thought about driving on by and letting the kids walk to school, but force of habit betrayed him, and he stopped. She got on the bus, and he had no choice but to shut the door and drive on.

Aunt Annie commenced to light into him something fierce. She dressed him down in a Christian way; then, having sermonized, she began to paganize. Some people can cuss you and you don't feel bad. Others can say something nice to your face, and you want to back up against the wall. Well, Aunt Annie could use words just like she used her sticking knife at the chicken plant. Buford said she sorta simmered down toward the end, and just trailed off saying she allowed as how the Methodist skirts warn't too clean either, and that was why the Methodist church in Blacksburg was God-forsaken and empty. By the time they got to school, all the kids trooped off to their classrooms, big-eyed, and with nary a word.

I'd rather have had Aunt Annie washing out my mouth with soap like she done Buford than have to be responsible for picking another preacher. If my Callie Mae was still with me, maybe she could have kept my mouth clear of the verbal diarrhea, but I had gotten in the habit of talking out loud to myself ever since she passed away, and when I got in public I sometimes forgot to notify my tongue.

When I studied history in college, I learned that a loose tongue was what caused a lot of it. We didn't know it right then, but we were on the verge of something historical right there in our own little corner of Arkansas.

So I made up my mind to be on that pulpit committee, since it looked like I was stuck. I decided right then that since age is no protection against foolishness, I'd not hold a preacher's age, or lack of it, agin him. As a matter of fact, I thought it might be a valuable resource for him to be young, so that when he got run off, he could stay out in front of the hatchet.

2

In View

Well, Millard's wife, Priscilla, cast our bread upon the waters and sent a letter down to that Baptist seminary in Texas asking them to send another sheep for our altar.

Having watched a few pulpit committees at work, or better than that, having known the people serving on those committees, the wording of the letter should have been something like, "Come preach in scrutiny of a call," rather than "in view of."

Not that that's all bad. It don't hurt none to "poke the pig" or "count the teeth" when you're shopping. We didn't do that last time, and you see where it got us. Nobody liked to talk about that, leastways in church. Millard said that's why they put me on the committee, seeing as how I was so close-mouthed and all.

By and by, someone took the bait. I was in Dolph's store getting some coal oil when the answer came. The letter was addressed to the church in care of Priscilla, and she read it to Millard while he sorted the rest of the day's mail into the cubbies. The "candidate" would be here in late March. That time of the year, there warn't really much to do to get ready for him—no grass to cut, windows to wash, or wasp

5

nests for the McAnelly twins to tear down, so we just waited to see what would heave into sight, ready to do our scrutinizing.

Aunt Annie started baiting her traps. It was a foregone conclusion that this prospect, just like all the others, would spend his first Saturday night with Wes and Annie so she could get first crack at him. About the only time I ever risked my friendship with Wes was when I suggested that the preacher stay at my place. Of course, I was just kidding—with Wes, that is; no one ever kidded Annie. Wes was a little mollified when I offered to help him sweep out the parsonage that week on the eve of our prospective preacher's visit. He warn't going to stay in it, but since the last preacher had left rather hastily, we thought we'd better make it presentable.

Down at Dolph's store Saturday morning, Wilbur, in one of his more optimistic bursts, said, "He better be married. We ain't going to have no wet-behind-the-ears preacher in our pulpit who ain't the husband of one wife, like the Bible says."

His brother Walter, who seldom goes to church, was getting his mail and overheard Wilbur. He said, "Wilbur, are you sure that's what you want? Paul didn't have a wife." He left, chuckling, having started the motor running. Wilbur fulminated for the next half hour to the empty air in defense of a married clergy. I'm not sure who he thought he was talking to—Walter was gone, and the rest of us had heard that song many times before. Truth be known, Wilbur was just wanting to make sure someone else suffered through matrimony like he had.

Well, they got here late that Saturday afternoon. I was watching the store for Dolph while he took his ulcer for a walk, so I was the first one to see them. Here came this skinny, burr-headed kid, who looked to me too young even to be in college, much less almost a seminary graduate. Beside him was a sweet-faced young woman in a plain cotton dress. He said, kind of timidly, "We're Gene and Sara Marshall. Could you tell us how to find Millard or Priscilla Doss?"

I said, "Sure, they run the post office in the back of the store. Come on in." I introduced myself, and kind of sized them up as we walked back to meet Priscilla. He wore Levis and cowboy boots, and I coulda sworn he walked a little bit bowlegged, like he actually had some acquaintance with the top side of a horse. She had bobbed brown hair, blue eyes, and had an air of sweet Southern gentility about her.

After we kind of walked around each other for awhile, Priscilla said, "We better get you on up to Aunt Annie's. She and Wes are expecting you, and that's where you'll be spending the night." What Priscilla didn't volunteer just then was the other main reason the preachers about to be viewed stayed at Wes and Annie's: Their house had one of the two indoor toilets in Blacksburg.

Like I said, it was March, and it blowed up a real fierce wind and rainstorm that night. Wes told me the next day that the thunder almost drowned out the preacher's snoring. He said that right after midnight he got up to go to the bathroom, and what with the lightning illuminating the house bright as day about every thirty seconds or so, it didn't make any difference that they didn't have electricity. He got to the bathroom door, which was open, about the same time that a boom and flash shook and lit the house.

There, ensconced on the commode, was Sister Sara in her nightgown, staring up in the blue light for a brief eternity at Wes in his long johns. She let out a scream, and Wes said, "Hush up, woman, what's the matter with you?" as he turned and beat a retreat to his bedroom. Sara, embarrassed and shaky, made her way back in the opposite direction, spooking and giving a little cry at every lightning flash.

Wes was afraid he'd gone and spoiled things for this preacher before he even had a chance to preach. But in a minute, he could hear a low tittering, followed by a medium-sized cackling, and then a backfire of muffled explosions of laughter from the front bedroom. Then things would get quiet, until the next lightning flash, when that ridiculous laughing spree would start over. After a second and third reprise, Wes began to smile. The rainstorm didn't bother Annie none, since she knew it warn't her equal, but when the giggle storm started, she pounded her pillow and said, "Go to sleep, Wes. How do you expect me to sleep with a grinning possum in my bed?"

Morning came, wet, clear, and sunny. Annie had already milked the cows when the preacher and his wife came to breakfast. "Did you all sleep well with all that racket last night?" she asked, ready to scold a couple of young folks for all that unholy carrying-on in her front bedroom.

Sara gave a quick glance at Wes, who reached for another biscuit, then checked with her husband, who was suddenly coughing into his napkin, and said, "Oh, yes, ma'am, that featherbed was just heavenly after that long drive yesterday. Did you make that beautiful quilt we slept under?"

Aunt Annie forgot about the scandalous cackling she had heard last night, filing it away for future use, if need be, and succumbed to the double-barreled load of flattery that hit her square in her tender spot—quilting. She almost cracked a smile as she answered proudly, "Shore did. I made the top this past winter, and the ladies in the quilting bee helped me quilt it. It's called a 'Friendship' quilt."

Wes told me he was reminded of this jasper who unscrewed and defused an unexploded bomb that had fallen in the ammo dump in his camp during the war. He didn't know what he was doing, and only the hand of God kept him from blowing himself and half of the battalion to smithereens. Wes said he knew Annie was a bomb about to blow, and Sara's question about quilting had been a neat job of defusing.

"Well," Annie said, "you 'uns better get on down to the church so you can meet everybody. Wes and I need to go by and pick up Granny.

You'll meet her later, since you'll be eating dinner there today."

Wes said that after the Marshalls left, Annie was speculating on whether Sister Sara would like to go to the next quilting bee. It was a real good sign.

THE CALL OF GOD

The preacher's first Sunday morning was sunny and a little windy—a good day for a sermon. Wes had just been telling me about the Marshalls's first Saturday night in Blacksburg, and we were finishing our cigarettes under the bean tree in the church's side yard when they rolled up in their blue 1952 Plymouth.

He looked a lot different in a suit, even if it was five years old like his car. Yesterday in blue jeans he was just a lanky, burr-headed kid who looked like he ought to be out lassooing stray cattle instead of stray sinners. Now he looked like a preacher, and (to our relief) even had a big, well-thumbed King James Version glued to his hand. He got out of the car and went around it to let his wife out.

"I guess the inside handle is broke, or something," Wes remarked.

We waved our nicotine-stained hands at them, and they waved back and started into the church. It was then I noticed their car rolling backwards. Of course, I could have run and set the brake for him, but the memory of that same kind of good deed was still too fresh in my mind.

I had gone to visit my Holiness cousin over at Ola last fall, and he talked me into going with him to this revival meeting at the brush arbor. We were loitering outside, listening to the cicadas, and practicing spitting, when the Holiness preacher came driving up. The preacher hopped out, praised the Lord, and headed into the brush arbor to pump up the lanterns. His car started rolling backwards, and helpful me, I hollered, "I'll get it!"

Well, I got it all right—stopped all good and proper, and I set the brake. But I broke the door handle off getting out of the car. See, there was this gunny sack wriggling on the floorboards, and I thought he had a couple of fryers in there to take home. I bent over to make sure they were getting air, and just barely touched that gunny sack when it almost exploded, flouncing all over the floor, accompanied with a whole orchestra of rattlesnake tail buzzing.

I do think that door handle was loose to begin with, though.

Not that I suspected this preacher prospect of ours of being a snake-handler, but I was practicing the security of the believer. Fortunately, the car stopped by itself when its back wheel bogged down in a mud puddle left from last night's rain.

They made a nice-looking couple, and the ladies and kids immediately crowded around Sister Sara. She was a good looker, and as it turned out, a real pretty singer after we taught her about shaped notes.

But don't go forming opinions about us, just because I said she was good-looking. I just couldn't help but think how much she reminded me of my daughter Dorothy, and was probably about the same age. We are very strait-laced around here. Sure, we have our opinions about the fair sex, and voice them, too, but at Blacksburg we reserve our comments for the single ladies. After they are married, the only compliments you hear about someone else's wife is with respect to their cooking, particularly pies. You compliment anyone's wife's pies, and the husband swells with pride like a happy toad. But you compliment anything else and you've got a big problem pronouncing certain words because you're minus some teeth.

Sara sang "Face to Face" before the sermon, and I think most everyone was ready to vote then, but of course we had to wait and hear the sermon. It warn't much, but I think he was just nervous. He stood stiff behind the pulpit and kept looking at his notes like he had never seen them before in his life. Wes said afterward, "If he could get his feet out of that basket, he would do better."

Wilbur said in a disappointed tone, "He didn't say nothing about whether Paul was married, or not."

Millard said, "Now, you all just heard a good message. He was just nervous, being in view of a call and all."

I had some reservations about calling a nervous kid to be our preacher. "Well, I'm not sure the church will vote to call him," I said, speaking mostly for myself.

Millard sure knew a lot. We kidded him about opening everybody's mail and reading all the secrets, but he may have just been that smart honestly. He looked at me and said, "Ollie, who do you think is calling who?"

"Why, I reckon that's plain," I answered. "We are. He came. We listened. Now we vote."

"That's only part of it, Ollie. You see, what if God is not a Democrat, like you think He is, and not white, like Dolph thinks He is, and is not asleep, like Ralph hopes and prays He is? The only way this preacher won't come is if He—" Millard glanced skyward, "—don't want him to come. And that's exactly why I hope this preacher does come. We need somebody who won't listen to every wheedling, whining, conniving sinner around here, but is interested in what God is saying."

We called him, and crossed our fingers.

4

Plum Jelly

We called, and they accepted. They had to go back to Fort Worth to get their things, but the very next week they returned to find the Ozarks in all their springtime splendor. When Preacher and Sara rolled over the mountain and looked down on the town of Blacksburg, I expect they had to stop to stuff their breath back in. I've lived here for many a year, and in the spring I still stop and gaze on all God's glory with awe and wonder. This part of Arkansas is purely heaven on earth, and on a spring morning, the horizontal bands of color define each ridge and mountain receding to the distant horizon, punctuated by vertical plumes of hickory smoke. Mount Nebo rises up blue in the south, and Petit Jean Mountain peeps over the ridge downriver. This time of the year, the smell of blossoms in the air vies with the aroma of fresh-turned soil and the hickorynut smell of scattered hogpens.

Early peaches were coming on, and the sheds were being opened and cleaned as the folks got ready for another season of peach harvest. Everybody old enough to smoke was either poised for work in the orchards or the sheds, or was already working in the chicken plant.

That is, of course, excepting the River men folks. None of them had ever worked in a peach shed, or at the chicken plant, which hired mostly women. But everyone at that slaughterhouse knew who they were, because they were always coming by there for entrails and fixin's for blood bait.

If you asked their wives, they would say those no-account males never worked a day in their lives, spending their days and nights lazing on the River, skulking after drum, carp, buffalo and cat by trotline. But if you asked them, they would testify they toiled, and would tick off as occupational hazards, "skeeters, snakes, snags, and sinking scows." Some of us town folk secretly envied this uncertain band of pilgrims who drifted forever in a haze of cigarette smoke and moonshine.

Town folk, farm folk, and River folk alike, Preacher quickly took to the land and to the people. It was a strange and wonderful honeymoon. Folks had never seen a grown man sleep past sunrise, lessen he was sick or drunk, and Preacher had never seen a people that went to bed so early you could still make out the clothesline from the back porch after the snoring started.

With everybody working, it was hard to find ministerial things to do between sermons, so Preacher checked the mail two or three times a day, nosed around a few stockponds to get acquainted with the elder denizens of the deep, and generally looked around for something to keep him busy. As an outlander he wouldn't have been allowed in the peach shed lines, and to tell the truth, he probably didn't think he could do it, after watching their speed and dexterity.

But he did know a thing or two about putting up fruit, because his mother had cooked and canned all through his growing-up years in Texas, and he and Sara needed a project. They decided to start with plums. Plums were a bumper crop that year, both the red and the yellow. Having selected a thicket of about a third of an acre near the church, Preacher and his wife crawled from one end to the other, harvesting every fallen plum to the tune of what turned out to be one hundred twenty-three Garrett and Red Rooster snuff jars full of jelly— enough to last through two and a half years of breakfast biscuits.

Since he was a newcomer to Arkansas, we expected a little bit of ignorance about our local wildlife. There was no way he could have known that plum thickets are the most favorite places for copperheads. Exactly how Preacher and Sister Sara never had a face-to-face meeting with some descendant from the Garden, only the inscrutable will of their joint Creator knew. I figured that it was either because this was Preacher's first church, and he hadn't acquired enough faith to shake a snake off into the fire like the Apostle Paul, or else God always takes care of widows, orphans, and idiots. I told Preacher later I would let him sort that out, since he was good at hermeneutics.

All of that came to light at Dolph's store about mail time one morning not long after he and Sister Sara had gotten settled in at the parsonage. Preacher brought a box of his plum jelly to give to whoever might be gathered there. Since work was in full tilt in the sheds, the recipients of his largess were the old-timers, the regulars, the hardened veterans of many a gospel campaign: Wes, Millard, Dolph, and me. We had been sharpening preachers right there in Dolph's store around the same potbelly stove for nigh on twenty years. It was time to start whittling on this new preacher kid.

"Hey, Preacher, you sure do have a passel of them jars there," said Dolph from behind the counter. "Do both you and your wife dip?"

"Hey, Preacher, you been trying out some of that Red Rooster yourself, so's you can get us a sermon ready for Sunday?" asked Wes, secretly pushing his own spit cup behind the chair leg with his heel.

Millard looked at him over the handful of letters he was sorting and chimed in, "Hey, Preacher, do you wash them jars before you load them up with jelly? That one looks a little brown in the bottom."

We didn't faze this Preacher—he had a humorous twist himself, and just gave it right back to us. He grinned and said, "I got some Red Rooster here that's already been chewed. It's good on biscuits—even dribbles down your chin good. Anybody want some?"

I took a jar of the red and said, "Hey, Preacher, when I was a young 'un, we used to play around in that same plum thicket I saw you in. That is, we did until one of the Riggs kids got taken."

Preacher looked at me kind of puzzled and asked, "What do you mean, 'taken'?"

"Well, we was having a rubber gun war around the Pumphrey barn near there, and the Riggs kid decided he would use some strategy. His folks had told him to stay out of that plum patch like ours had done us, but he halfway disbelieved them, and anyways, war was calling. So he bellied his way through the thicket to sneak up on us, and he got taken."

"Oh, you mean there was an accident?"

"Naw, it warn't no accident. He stuck his ever-lovin' nose right into the face of a fat copperhead—what that snake did was purely intentional. It tagged old James in the face pretty fierce before he caterwauled out of there. Old Doc Scoggins at Clarksville did what he could, but how do you put a tourniquet on the head? Around the nose, or around the neck? Anyways, he died, and not very purty, neither. The next day the grownups went stomping through that thicket with their shoes on, gingerlike, to see where it happened, and there was that old snake in the very place, coiled up beside the unfired rubber gun, waiting for another engagement from the enemy. Well, someone had brought his shotgun, and took care of that snake good and proper. That was nigh on fifty years ago, and no one ever went near that place again. That is, not until you hove into town."

Preacher searched for a consonant to go with the vowels he was handling, failed, and slid to the floor in a faint. The Red Roosters preceded him, and several broke, leaving a gooey mass of red and yellow jelly splattered around. Wes pulled Preacher out of the mess, muttering, "I thought this 'un was a Baptist, but it shore looks like he's leaning Pentecostal, rolling around on the floor like this, and in public, too."

Millard slapped his unposted letters down on the counter, and lamented, "Doggone your mouth, Ollie! Now who's gonna clean up this mess?"

5

SWAPPING

Right after that jelly episode, Wilbur came huffing into the store one morning, muttering about that Texas seminary not tending to Baptist distinctives. That didn't mean a thing, except that Wilbur had his nose out of joint about something Preacher did or didn't do. Wilbur got his mail and went on down to Wes's to borrow his lespedeza spreader, mumbling something about his pocket knife. The mention of a pocketknife told me what I needed to know. I had a chore to do.

So after the mail train had run, and Preacher came in, without any jelly this time, and looking kind of sheepish, I told him to stay awhile and talk. What I meant was for him to stay awhile and listen to a little extemporaneous sermonizing of my own.

I said, "Preacher, I want to tell you about these people here in the Bend—you've got to start using a little discernment with them. Otherwise, you're going to be cold-shouldered right out of this left-hand corner of heaven. You just refused to trade knives with Wilbur, didn't you?"

He looked at me like I was plumb out of my mind and said, "Well, of course I did. You should have seen that bent-up old pocketknife he wanted to trade me for my good Camus."

I shook my head and said, "You just don't know what you did when you turned down his offer to swap. You done flunked your first exam in preacherin' in Blacksburg. Didn't Jesus eat with sinners? Didn't he drink water out of the same cup as Hot Lips Lucy of Sychar? Well, it ain't going to hurt you none to do a little swapping with us folks, and Wilbur in particular. Have you ever seen that cigar box Wilbur has in his front room? Well, it's full of knives, every blessed kind and value of knife from frog stickers to Old Timer chaw knives."

"So what?" he asked, with a nervous little shrug.

"What do you mean, 'So what?' Preacher, you are some kind of dense. Have you never heard of Joshua and his stone pickers? How they picked up stones crossing Jordan, and he said, 'Whenever your smart aleck kids say "So what," you tell them about these stones.' Let me tell you, them knives is to Wilbur what them stones was to Joshua.

"You don't know what Wilbur's doing, but he does. I do, and Dolph and Millard and Wes, and all of us here in the Bend. But you—you come high-falutin' up here out of Texas and don't know the first thing about the high calling of Swap. Don't you realize that God is a swapper? Didn't He say, 'Come on, let's dicker—you lay down your best, and I'll lay down my best, and I'll tell you what, I'll swap with you.' Well, if you ain't read that, you ain't read Isaiah lately. Anyhow, Wilbur is one of your deacons, and he's got a knife in that box for every preacher and evangelist that has ever lived here or held a meeting here."

Preacher looked at me kind of sideways and asked, "What for?"

"Why, he reads character when he trades, that's what he does. He reads swappers' souls like you read your Greek. When you say you won't swap, you're saying, 'I'm a shut-up book, nobody is going to read me.' And if you intend to be a real preacher, you have got to learn that people need to read you as much as they do the Good Book. You may not like it none, but you are the front porch to the house of God, and if you want folks coming in, they're going to have to walk through and over you, clean their feet off on you, spit on you, sit and enjoy the view with you—know you, or they never will go in the house.

"When you trade with Wilbur, you are saying, 'Come up on my porch, I ain't got nothing to hide.' So what if he does slick you out of a good Camus for a nicked Barlow, and brags about it later? You have gained a brother—and a deacon."

Preacher nodded his head, like some of this was soaking in.

"By the way," I added, half serious and half funning, "you wouldn't want to trade that deep sea tackle I saw hanging in your carport, would you?"

"Well," he said, and his lip curled up a little, "let's see what you got."

I grinned and said, "Preacher, you might do okay after all."

6

LORD'S SUPPER

It all started out peaceful enough, that first hot Sunday night in late spring after Preacher came. He was positioning the elements of his first Lord's Supper with all the care of Aaron casting lots before the Lord.

He arranged and rearranged the soda crackers (which didn't have enough salt in them to suit me) and the sniffers of Welch's grape juice on the table in front of the pulpit. I wondered if all that moving around of the Body and Blood had some additional spiritual significance, and I meant to ask Millard about it later. The ordinance was still a novelty to some of us, enough so that us old codgers were there way before services started, to check out what that Texas seminary taught nowadays. We were particularly entranced to see how Preacher would handle the cover cloth.

When Preacher had everything in place, I gave the Masonic sign to Wes, who turned on the attic fan. Said fan was directly above the pulpit. The altar cloth seemed to tremble a little bit, then it gathered its skirts and headed for the ceiling. Preacher did a masterful job of snatching that thing right out of the air, but his sermon notes, which were on the pulpit, were sacrificed to the rapture.

Preacher reset the stage with a songbook holding down each corner of the cloth. "Jest like that last preacher done," Wes whispered to Millard and me. "I guess Modernism hasn't hit Fort Worth after all."

Latecomers probably thought Preacher was casting glances towards Heaven, but us early birds knew better: We could see various pages of his sermon notes sucked against the screen of the attic fan overhead. Wes whispered again to Millard and me, "Maybe he'll get his feet out of the basket tonight, without them notes. What do you think?"

Well, just in time for the start of the service, in walked one of them Church of Christers from Flat Rock. He had on dark blue pants and work shirt, sleeves down, collar buttoned, and the zeal of God written all over him. He didn't take a seat, but marched right down front to where Preacher was standing at the table. I've noticed that preachers in general get this hopeful look every time someone gets within six feet of the front. Well, our Preacher warn't no different. I guess he thought he had him a convert even before the service started, which would have been providential, seeing as how his sermon had already been delivered and received on high. But it didn't take long to go from the gates of heaven to the smoky regions—that Flat Rocker lit into the Antichrist (Preacher), the Great Whore (the Baptist church), the piano (tool of the devil), and the Table (something about a card game, "euchre," I think he called it).

A couple of us had surreptitiously moved up a couple of rows so we could hear Preacher gulp better. He had plenty of time to recover, though, since the tirade was longer than a Baptist Young People's Union part, read laboriously by some earnest and determined victim with a third grade education.

I think Preacher was on the horns of a dilemma. If no one else had been there, he probably would've offered an evening sacrifice in holy joy. As it was, he was under the eye of his flock, and had to display all the Christian virtues, even though at the moment he couldn't remember what they were exactly—only that they ran counter to what he wanted to do. You might have thought that this was a good place for that old adage of "discretion being the better part of valor," or, if you had hung around the Bend a few years, you probably would have said, "After a couple of tries of sticking your foot in the hay baler, you sorta get discouraged."

Well, Preacher looked kinda discouraged after trying to butt in with some doctrine of his own for the third time, but that Flat Rocker had a head of steam. Then from the back row came a third, but not disinterested party. Aunt Annie was almost as big as a dirtdobber, and didn't weigh much over a hundred pounds carrying a ten pound sack of sugar. She had been heard to laugh once, according to Dolph, but no one had actually seen her smile. She warn't choosing this night to begin, neither. She waded into the deep water between Preacher and the Pharisee and let fly. I reckon that kind of language hadn't been heard in Blacksburg since they churched (other denominations say *un*churched) fifty-four people for siding with the family of a female Sunday School teacher who had gone dancing one Saturday night back in the forties. No swearing or cussing, you understand: just deadly, vicious, verbal knife sticking it was. Several of us turned to look at Wes—he was grinning and punctuating certain phrases with emphatic nods.

It seemed that our visitor was one of those River john-boaters who sold fish on the weekend in Russellville, and got his entrails and blood fixin's at the Clarksville chicken plant (or *poultry* plant, as the high school graduates in town say). Our zealot finally got his eyes off the Antichrist and focused on his new adversary, and then he recognized her. The holy fire went out in his eyes just like someone had blowed out a candle. He crawfished backwards until he bumped into the first pew, then edged sideways into the aisle, where he was escorted to the front door on a flowery bed of verbal nightshade and hemlock. Annie skittered first on one side of him, then the other, making sure she filled both ears equally.

Preacher asked Millard next morning at mail call how come Aunt Annie got such a clutch hold on the Flat Rocker. Millard explained, "Oh, didn't you know? Annie's the 'sticker' at the chicken plant." Seeing the puzzled look on Preacher's face, he continued. "You know, they hang the chickens up by the legs on a conveyor belt, and they get run by this person with an electric prod, who 'stuns' them. Then they run by the 'sticker,' who takes off the heads. That's Annie, and she comes home with blood on her every night. She's pretty good with a knife. Our visitor last night decided not to jeopardize his connection to the best bait store in the county . . . not even for a verity of the faith."

We noticed that Preacher laid off preaching anything that would miff the Woman's Missionary Union after that, seeing as how Annie was president. And there was a big crowd the next time we had the Lord's Supper, but, like most sequels, it warn't up to par.

7

GOIN' HOME

Preacher's first funeral happened to coincide with the inaugural of the new Goin Funeral Home in Clarksville. We should've guessed that things would get out of hand with a name like that doing the honors. Not that a man should be ashamed of his name, but there are some names that are an open invitation for ridicule. Goin Home would've made the list without their name, if you know what I mean, or you will when you hear the rest.

Their client and our deceased was a wizened little bitty old lady from up around Horsehead Lake. Nobody seemed to know her very well until after the funeral, but her kin were pretty visible folks. The daughters showed up at every election, hollering "Foul!" They threw popcorn at every home basketball game. And they circulated petitions for everything from lower electric rates, to the Hoxsey Cancer Clinic, to larger school lunches. We figured they must've had a mother somewheres, but we didn't know this was her. Wes, who, like his wife, warn't much bigger than a dirtdobber, said at the wake, "I'd shrink up, too, if I had a Tom Fool family like that."

The Goin Home people hadn't organized their act very well, but it seemed to come off. They carried the casket up the church steps—thirteen, there was. (I've been around Arkansas, Oklahoma, and parts of Texas a good bit, and I notice that Baptist, even Methodist, churches almost always have thirteen steps. I don't know why that is, and I'm a thirty-second-degree Mason.) When they got her through the door, they rolled her down to the front.

Some of the great theological battles of our time are whether to have open or shut caskets, whether to open them after the service, should the head be to the right or left, should the preacher precede or follow the casket out, and should the preacher eat seconds at the funeral meal. I understand every age in Christianity had its peculiar battles against heresy, and ours is no different. Now, I'm very much for orthodoxy, and when it comes to leaving this world, a proper send-off is real important.

Well, Preacher did pretty good. I've seen oldtimers try to work up a few tears while preaching over their friends and have to really rub and work to get anything flowing. But Preacher not only cried, he actually choked and blubbered a little bit, and he didn't even know the deceased. That's pretty good.

Finally, the time came to quit. Preacher was done, and kept shifting his Bible from hand to hand, waiting for the Goin folks to come do their part. Wes finally had to get up and go get the funeral directors, who were outside under a tree, having a smoke. Looking slightly aggrieved, they came down the aisle with a light blue Bull Durham trail following them, and busied themselves arranging the few flowers, opening the casket, and spreading the muslin net over the open casket.

I noticed the net spreader look up at Preacher with a pained expression on his face, but Preacher had on his Seminary look—the one staring down the corridors of Eternity to the very throne of God, and the poor mortal was unable to catch his eye. He cast his eyes left and right for help, and seeing none, he scurried back down the aisle to where Mr. Goin was standing at the rear, still ruminating over the full cigarette he had had to jettison. After a whispered confab, Mr. Goin hurried to the front, looked in the casket, and thundered, "My God! She's gone!"

The family stood in unison. The youngest daughter screamed, the middle daughter did a theatrical half turn and swooned, and Mamie, the eldest, rushed to the casket for verification, where she stood working her jaws for a bit, then let loose with, "She's been raptured! She's been *RAPTURED!*"

Preacher, in the meantime, made do with shifting his Bible from hand to hand, broke his gaze down the eternal corridors of time, and in total amazement looked down with unbelieving eyes and ears. As Mamie hollered, "She's been raptured!" she hammered out a litany on the lower part of the casket lid, and the excitement got to Preacher. He suddenly upchucked right there—and sprayed Mamie, the casket, the flowers, and all in one vast upheaval. The only one to miss out was the deceased, who had slid down to the foot end of the casket during the thirteen-step ascent.

"My God!" came the benediction from Mr. Goin.

Several weighty theological issues were settled that day. Goin Funeral Home learned that the scriptural way to carry a casket is feet first, so the corpse won't slide out of sight going up steps. I got a special insight as to why thirteen is an unlucky number. And Preacher, he learned to wait until after the service to have the funeral meal. Everybody else seemed to think that was a good idea, too.

Maybe that's how religious orthodoxy came to be in the first place.

SNAKES

We were having pretty good crowds at church on Sundays. Preacher worked hard, digging something new out of his Bible garden, and he did a good job serving it. It didn't hurt none, though, that he had this string of unlikely disasters beating his drum. I understand the Bible says people followed the Apostles to see what miracles they would do. People in Blacksburg followed Preacher just to see what the little cloud over his head would produce next. Me, I wouldn't have missed a service for the world.

Preacher was very mission-minded—wanted to "go to the field" himself someday. I never understood that, seeing as this town of fewer than two hundred could stir up enough sin to keep this or any preacher busy full time. If he didn't get tired of preaching agin it, we wouldn't get tired of producing it.

Anyways, he invited missionaries to speak as often as he dared. Some said that if he didn't preach, he oughtn't to get paid, so he had to use discretion. Our change of pace one Sunday night in early summer was Brother Cullen, a missionary from South America. He came with all his bells and whistles. Loren and Zane, the McAnelly twins, helped him unload his boxes and bags on Sunday afternoon, and arrange them before the pulpit in preparation for the services later that day. The twins seemed as interested in missions as Preacher. They lingered to study the boxes in awe, wondering what was in them.

That evening, all the Woman's Missionary Union ladies, led by Aunt Annie, corralled the Girls' Auxiliary girls and the Royal Ambassador boys and a few miscellaneous kids who warn't nothing, up to the front rows, and there they sat with great anticipation as the missionary uncovered his displays for view. There was a huge, rolled-up snake skin, a pair of drums, an ominous hornet's nest still attached to a branch, and the usual shrunken heads. Dolph allowed as how they were probably deacons' heads, but Millard said, "No, they couldn't be deacons, because their mouths are too small, and they're sewed shut."

Brother Cullen started telling about his adventures in the Amazon, using his collection of visual aids. He pulled the stopper on the hornet's nest and said to the front rows of kids, "What would you do in the jungle, if you bumped into a nest like this, and out came a stream of angry hornets?" Brother Cullen suddenly started making strange movements. We supposed it was a tribal dance, or maybe a new preacher's gesture that we hadn't seen yet. First he fidgeted, then he shivered, then he scratched his head with one hand, then he gave up and threw down the nest and scratched his head, armpits, and places that oughtn't to be scratched in polite company. I'm not certain how they did it, but only the McAnelly twins could have managed it—somehow they had stuffed that hornet's nest with chicken mites.

One of the RAs, thinking that the Great White Father was caught up in a tribal dance, entered into the spirit of things and grabbed a drumstick and laid it to the drums. One of them gave an authentic jungle *boom*. The other had a loose drumhead, and it came off after one blow and set loose a troop of scurrying tarantulas, slightly addled by the first reverberation. Whether they can hear or not is debatable, but they were certainly put through the test by the congregation, both low pitch and high pitch.

About that time, Aunt Annie sang out, "Lookee, that snake skin is moving!" And it was—something was rolled up in it. Preacher didn't think so, I guess, because he unrolled it with a great flourish like a red carpet. Later he told me that Brother Cullen had told him to do that when he gave the signal. Brother Cullen was giving so many signals that Preacher got confused. Well, those twins had tour-de-forced themselves. Rolled up in that snake skin, and now tumbled out on the floor, was a passel of bullsnakes, and they hit the floor running. Most of the WMU ladies hustled themselves up onto the pews, hollering, but Aunt Annie went into action for God and for country. Standing on the rostrum were the stalwart and dusty American and Christian flags, which she grabbed forthwith, and lambasted every one of those snakes with the butt end of the poles before they made it to the third row of pews. She warn't exactly silent while she did it, neither. Whether they died of burst eardrums or broken spinal columns was a toss-up. All the while, Preacher never moved; he stayed up on the rostrum, still gripping the snake skin.

Some folks driving by out front stopped and came in. They told Wes that they thought they heard a lady preacher inside and had stopped to see if this was the Holiness church. Wes said, "Naw, it's just my wife, Annie, putting the fear of God into those snakes."

The newcomer responded, "That's what I thought. This is the place, and they're handling snakes tonight. Let me go get my family and bring them in."

The next Sunday night, Preacher started preaching through Acts, but he skipped the part about Paul getting bit by a snake and shaking it off into the fire.

9

TROPHIES OF GRACE

Lightning don't strike the same place twice. Uh-huh. And taxes ain't going up next year. Our candidate, if elected, is gonna put all those rascals out of office. Open wide, this won't hurt. I done turned the breaker off. You get my drift? Well, we done disproved that wisdom about lightning once and for all, when not more than two Sundays later, we had another missionary speaker. It warn't Brother Cullen—he was bound back to the Amazon, amongst the pythons and the headhunters, but far away from the McAnelly twins.

This one was Brother Crossnoes, and he had come to speak about the needs down at the Little Rock Orphanage. By his tell of it, he was an orphan himself, and grew up in the Indian Lands, somewhere near where Trousdale is now, except it ain't there no more. It disappeared about the time they quit using Delco for power. He brought some good exhibits with him—pictures of long-haired, skinny-necked kids, standing woebegone and barefoot in the dead of winter. Looking at those pictures, which he passed around, gave everybody there a queasy feeling—some out of sympathy for a benighted child, some out of personal experience, and some out of the realization that they were about to see their hard-earned sale and swap money heading for Little Rock.

That was just the beginning. Next, we heard about the early days, the dark time of no food, no fires, short sheets, mean foster parents. Then came the "shining light in the darkness" (none other than our pulpit guest), his noble sacrifices, his long years of making do to keep the wolf from the door, the devil at bay, and the kids from perdition. Finally, he related several grand stories about some of their "graduates," who had gone on to "bless society, uplift the churches, and further the Kingdom."

Wes leaned over and whispered to me, "That Southern gentleman could've been elected governor of Vermont in 1870." I agreed, and just hoped he wouldn't come back again right after crops were cashed in, or after peach harvest. In fact, I hoped he wouldn't come back at all.

But he warn't quite through. He had brought two "trophies of grace" with him, the clinching nails for our coffin lid. One of them had polio and wore a crutch. The other coughed in long spasms that belonged in *Ripley's Believe It or Not.* He called them up to stand beside him on the rostrum, his "dear little brothers and angels." That took about ten minutes, one wobbling and coughing up the steps, the other struggling on his crutch, and falling twice.

The second time he fell, Preacher jumped up to help him, and I would swear that the little angel jabbed his crutch at him; but then, maybe not. Preacher was a little awkward anyway, and probably just happened to get his crotch in the way. Preacher kind of hunched over and shuffled backwards to his seat while these poor little suffering lambs finally made it up to where they could gaze lovingly up at their shepherd.

These would have made dandy pictures to show somewheres else, except for what happened next.

First, you have to know that Blacksburg is about halfway from Little Rock to Fort Smith, so travelers have to stop and roost somewhere. In the old days, it meant stopping at Toadsuck Ferry the first night, then Pottsville Inn, Spadra, or Altus the next night. But nobody stopped at Blacksburg. If they were traveling on the River, they might stop near there at Pittsburg, but not at Blacksburg. Anyone spending the night at Blacksburg had to be too cheap for the inns, or a real conniver in wheedling out a night's lodging and two meals from some poor sucker in the Bend.

The River bends south of Blacksburg. They call it The Bend, and like all sacks and pokes, it tends to gather odds and ends in the bottom that just never get flushed out to move on down or up the River. Telling all this now is relevant, because all the Bend people came in to hear about the Orphanage that night. One was Widow Scaggs and her four-year-old boy from down past the Bend cemetery. They was sitting at the back, where they was more comfortable, and so was the WMU. I can be a man of few words, and on that subject, I just said 'em.

While the "trophies of grace" were singing their Song of Ascents, Wes punched me and pointed. Widow Scaggs had moved to the outside aisle and had run the gauntlet of Aunt Annie and the rest of the WMU to get a seat closer to the front.

What happened then didn't seem like proper timing—kind of like sitting at the table, saying grace, then leaving the table without even passing the greens. Brother Crossnoes saw Widow Scaggs moving toward the front, stared at her and the boy, and said quickly, "Let us pray."

People bowed their heads—most of them, anyway—and some who did kept one eye forward. I, for one, thought, "He's not even going to take an honest offering . . . he's going to frisk our pockets while our eyes are shut."

Then, like the voice of an archangel, came a loud "No! You stay right where you are, you lecher!"

It was Widow Scaggs, all right. It sure sounded like she knew him, and to look at his stricken face, it sure looked like he knew who she was. And it looked like he was about to rapture himself out of some serious tribulation, 'cause he was already three steps down toward the side door. The events that followed were not too spiritual. While "Widow" Scaggs and Brother Crossnoes were scuffling on the rostrum, the two "trophies" were running around lightfooted and loose as fairies, and the four-year-old was hollering, "Mommy, is that my daddy?"

Preacher was going up and down with his hands like a choir director with no choir, but no one paid him any mind. It was the sheriff who gave the benediction that night, when he led Brother Crossnoes off to the county hoosegow, and told everyone to get on home, the show was over.

Like Dolph says, "It takes a fool to think he can stick his foot in a hay baler twice and not get discouraged." Seems that our Brother Crossnoes had worked the Bend about four years and nine months ago, when he had some different kind of ministry going.

The next morning, some reporters from the *Gazette* and the *Democrat* came up from the Big City to interview Preacher. But they had to wait until Aunt Annie got finished with her say.

10

STORM CELLAR

It was the dead heat of summer, and the air was heavy and ominous with change, the same way a powder keg is when the burning fuse gets short. Down in the Bend they had been working from the time the dew burned off till late-thirty for days on end, racing to get the hay crop in before the weather changed. The men were irritable, the horses wild-eyed, the children subdued; and the women worked in secret fear, one eye on their men and the other on the sky. So there warn't many at prayer meeting that Wednesday night—just Preacher, the older women, a few young tykes, and us old codgers.

Now don't go making any assumptions about us old codgers. Prayer meeting was not our forte. Ever since I can remember, prayer meeting was for the preacher, women, kids, and one or two deacons to keep tabs on the faith. But somebody had to be there, what with Flat Rockers trying to bust up the meeting, or some shyster sharpening his repertoire on the gullibles. Like Millard always said, "We are the true defenders of the faith."

We were somewheres on the Sea of Galilee, about verse twelve, when a tremendous clap of thunder rattled through the open south windows, circled the room a couple of times, and left out the north windows. Now, I usually sit on the aisle so I can lean one arm on the end and sorta stretch my legs into the aisle. I just barely got them retracted before Sister Myrtle came whizzing down the aisle, heading for the exit and her storm cellar. I could've just left my legs there, 'cause she hurdled where they had been.

About then we heard the eight o'clock freight coming like it always does in the middle of the Sunday night sermon (the tracks run right close to our south windows). This bothered Preacher something fierce when he first arrived, making him lose his train of thought. He got to where he used the time to study his notes and pick up points he'd skipped over, and by the time the caboose clicked by, he was ready to go again. It seemed like two sermons sometimes. Millard said he preached the Old Testament before the train came, then let the caboose carry the Spirit and the Bride away.

Then somebody realized that this was Wednesday night, not Sunday, and the train didn't run on Wednesday. Only three things make a noise like a train, and two of them is trains. We were listening to number three, which was a tornado headed straight for prayer meeting.

People started getting up in a reverse domino theory. If Preacher had had a door behind the choir, he could have given an invitation then and made his fellow preachers green with envy at the next Associational meeting. My feet warn't in nobody's way that time. I was busy leading people out, and off to the races we went. Everybody knew exactly where they were going, and how long it would take to get there. Except Preacher. Poor Preacher didn't believe in storm cellars. Part of that was probably his mortal fear of scorpions and centipedes, which just reminded him of snakes. He called out to the retreating army, "We need to exercise faith and trust in the Lord!"

I looked back once, and there was Preacher framed in the doorway, looking sort of uncertain. Sister Sara was off visiting her folks, so he didn't have no one to tell him what to do.

I always try not to be the last one to get in the storm cellar. This is, in part, so I can set a good example: We don't want to raise a bunch of slouches around here. Besides, if I get there first, I can check for snakes or broken fruit jars. So I didn't see which way Preacher went. There were plenty of places to go—every yard had a cellar, except the parsonage. When he finally decided to duck in someone's cellar to keep his sermon notes dry, he had the bad luck to stumble into Sister Haseltine's.

Now Jeannie Haseltine didn't trust preachers, a feeling she shared with a lot of folks. She was a little peculiar, but we all liked her, knowing what she had been through. Rupert, her husband, had been dead for twenty years; the first ten above ground, the last ten after the Sheriff pronounced him ready for a funeral. Those ten years dead above ground, he spent likkered up most of the time, persecuting Jeannie, and ranting on about a treasure he and his brother Jesse had found up near Hagarville in an Indian cave. Jesse had every reason to want Jeannie to have the benefit of it, but Rupert had made him swear secrecy on his Masonic apron, and he took the secret to his grave. That sorta fixed it until Rupert died (the time when he quit living and we buried him).

We first noticed lantern light peeping out of the storm cellar door cracks one night not long after the funeral. Wes and I were walking home from the Lodge and crept up close—not into the yard, just up by the fence—and could hear somebody in the cellar. We heard somebody moving dirt, and mixed in between shovel loads, a kind of quiet, desperate crying, like some wounded thing. Wes was kind of big-eyed anyway, but his eyes just about outbugged themselves before we beat it for home.

It warn't long before everybody knew what was going on in that cellar. Jeannie would hide her hands when she came to the post office, and we noticed her shoes were really broke down. I reckon the dirt in that storm cellar was about the most pulverized dirt in the whole county, and the least productive. But she kept after it. There was a fortune somewhere in that dirt floor; she just hadn't found it yet.

Liza thought she would get a peek down that cellar when she took six quarts of green beans over one day. She said, "Jeannie, I thought you might enjoy these. Could I maybe get some empties out of your cellar, and you just keep these?"

"No!" said Jeannie, with eyes as big as Wes's. "No, ma'am, there ain't no jars down there. They was all broke, and I threw them down the old dry well."

All it cost Liza to find out that Jeannie wouldn't let no one look in that cellar was six quarts of beans. One itinerant preacher (before Preacher came) paid with his hide. He tried to bamboozle his way into the cellar, and Jeannie hied him over the tracks with her hoe. That didn't endear preachers to Jeannie, but then, she had never been to church anyway, what with Rupert being dead above ground so long. Now all Jeannie cared about was Rupert's only legacy to her—his treasure.

Well, that was where the Urim and Thummin took Preacher on that stormy night. When he told us the story later, he said he just headed for the first open storm cellar he could see. He fell over a shovel on the steps, and measured himself on the dirt floor, but it was a soft landing. When Jeannie saw Amahl the Night Visitor sniffing the dirt, practically breathing on her treasure, she lit on him like a panther. We were battened down several storm cellars away, but we could hear this banshee cry rising and falling. Wes and I looked at each other, and he said, "I wish that woman would hush, so we could hear the storm."

The storm passed about as quick as it had blown up, but Preacher was the only one to take a direct hit. In fact, he had taken several. We got him patched up and his clothes washed before his wife got back.

The next day, when Preacher came into Dolph's store to get the mail, Millard said, "Well, Preacher, what you gonna preach on this Sunday—'A Night with the Witch of Endor'?"

Preacher grinned and said, "No, but do you mind if I post my sermon topics here by the door?"

After he left, we crowded around to see what he had pinned up. His topics for the next four Sunday nights were:

The Pearl of Great Price
The Servant Who Buried His Talent
Seek, and Ye Shall Find
The Secret of True Riches

Well, I thought that was a little underhanded, hanging all those juicy worms on a gospel hook, but it worked. Jeannie came to every one of those Sunday night services, and she got converted. I bet old Rupert drilled himself right out of his coffin, spinning in his grave.

MAKING THE GRADE

Blacksburg had always gotten a seasoned preacher before, but this new one from Texas had never been ordained. He'd had his first funeral in our church, and held his first Lord's Supper in our church, but his ordination was going to be a first, both for Preacher and for us.

Sister Sara worried a lot about that coming day. When they first got here, Preacher had a burr haircut. We didn't know that was all he had ever had since the sixth grade. I guess Sara heard Elmo or Annie talking one day about how he looked too young to be an ordained preacher, and that galvanized her into action—nothing would do but for Preacher to let his hair grow out. She didn't have to be told that her husband needed all the respectability he could get—particularly since so many undignified things seemed to happen around him, and most of them on Sunday. At first, Preacher balked at the idea of having hair too long to comb with a washrag. He probably had some inner sense telling him no good would come of it, but finally he relented.

Church over the next several months was something to behold—

or at least, Preacher was. That hair of his, once it rared up, became the focus of everyone's eye. Even the Junior boys, who were proving their manhood by moving from the front row to sit at the back with the men, gave up and moved back to the front so they could see it better.

Sara bit her nails over how slow the transformation took. As his hair passed the overgrown lawn stage and entered the waving sheaves of grain dispensation, Preacher noticed the rapt attention of young and old alike. He thought his sermons must really be getting good. Wilbur and Elmo shook their heads and called the Associational Missionary, Brother Eben Dothan, and asked him to postpone the ordination until the preacher's hair could show some inclination toward the horizontal rather than the vertical.

Preacher's tonsure became a community effort. Dolph gave him an old silk stocking from the store and showed him how to knot it into a tight nightcap. Preacher would carefully begin at his face and pull that thing on so that his hair would run straight back. I bet he had trouble sleeping at first, with that unrelenting grip on his scalp threatening to carry his eyebrows up to the top of his skull.

Wilbur, who lived near the parsonage, got up every morning to drive his cow in for milking. It would have been easy for him to walk straight through the pasture to Old Bossy, but he developed the habit of taking the long way around, which took him through Preacher's side yard, and past the screened-in back porch where Preacher and Sister Sara slept in the hot summer months. Of course, the real reason was to see if the preacher was still in bed.

After several nights of fitful sleep wearing that silk suction cup, Preacher slept longer than usual one morning. When Wilbur came by, he peered in and saw a mound in the bed, so he raked a stick on the screen and called out, "Preacher, air you up yet?"

Preacher sat bolt upright in the bed, startled into instant wakefulness. Wilbur saw him with his silk cap on through the screen and said, "Lord-a-mercy, there's a Chinaman in Sister Sara's bed!" and beat a hasty retreat. He forgot to milk Old Bossy that morning.

Preacher jerked the nightcap off, tugged his eyes and eyebrows back onto his face, and exclaimed, "That does it! No more!"

Later, while he was down at the store fuming around, Slim gave him a little jar of Butch, which I think was designed to help people's hair stand up, but in Preacher's case it was hoped it could be used to make his hair lay down. Anything was worth a try.

It seemed to help, though Sister Sara had to wash a lot of pillow-cases. It also added another dimension to the preaching service. Preacher would march over from the parsonage very carefully, speak to the people out front and as he came down the aisle, all the while with a nice wet-looking, plastered-down head of hair. During the progress of Point One of the sermon, he would remember the situation, but along about Point Two, Point Three, or the closing Poem or Illustration, he would forget himself, and start adding animation to his face.

That was when it happened. A wrinkled brow, a smile, just about anything would trigger it—"it" being the roostertail in his hair, right at the crown. Then following in due course, the dried-out hairs, encouraged by their predecessors, would rise up one by one. Of course, the kids were delighted, Sara was mortified, Wilbur and Elmo chagrined (they thought he did it on purpose), and Wes and I . . . well, we had a hard time being religious.

Heretic hair or no, this was our Preacher, and the day of his ordination finally arrived. I knew in my heart of hearts that there was no possible way that it could end up being a "normal" ordination, not with Preacher involved.

An ordaining council was assembled, including eleven preachers from as far away as the other end of the next county, and Brother Eben Dothan. There was also Brother Trueblood from Harmony, over near Fort Smith, whom Preacher had asked to come and preach the Ordination Sermon. I suppose it's natural for preachers what came up the hard way, or were called late in life, and had little formal education (certainly none in a seminary), to look with a jaundiced eye at the "new kind" of preacher being cranked out of the Texas seminary. But they all made sure to come, even though they had to get home to preach on Sunday night.

The whole faithful flock was there, too. I think we were all nervous, because we didn't know what was supposed to happen. We were developing into a nervous church anyway, what with almost every Sunday serving up a new dish. We started out with singing at two o'clock, and then the thirteen members of the ordaining council adjourned to Preacher's front room. The rest of the people stayed in the church and sang hymns, with a few sneaking out now and then to roll a smoke, or go over to Preacher's to use the indoor bathroom.

That last item is why Wes and I were over at the parsonage—Wes was stationed at the front door, which represented the beeline approach to the bathroom from the church, and also the doorway to the ordaining council. Wes was supposed to herd those being called by nature around back, where I would usher them in through the back door and down the hall to the bathroom, standing guard to make sure none of them exited through the front room.

I was doing a steady line of business for awhile, but when things slowed down, and the commode tank quit running, it dawned on me I had a pretty good position for listening to what was going on in the ordaining council. Now, I don't eavesdrop—that's putting your ears to the door or wall and cupping your hand. I learned not to do that at the Lodge. All I was doing was my duty, and I couldn't help it if preachers talk loud.

Evidently they had Preacher sitting in a chair with a semicircle of questioners giving it to him hot and heavy. It didn't sound like everyone was participating, but that they had a couple of ringleaders: I recognized the voice of Brother Dacus from Ola (the one with a nasal twang), and Brother Hartreader from Plainview. Brother Hartreader was asking Preacher what he thought about the ordinances, how many there were, and so on.

I began to realize that Preacher knew more about the Bible than any of his questioners, and my chest started swelling with pride. I wanted to run out and tell Wes to come go to the bathroom, or something, so he could hear. But about then, Brother Dacus said, "Brother Marshall, let me ask you, if the time ever comes when you don't believe like the rest of us Baptists, will you turn in your ordination certificate?"

Well, Preacher didn't like that one, I guess. He told Brother Dacus to explain what he meant, "believe like the rest of us." Apparently that's one thing you don't do when you're a candidate—ask a question yourself. Brother Dacus blustered and said, "I'll do the asking here. What will you do if you don't agree with our Baptist faith and message?"

I forgot all about Wes, and my throat got a little dry as I heard Preacher stand up and say, "Brother Dacus, I'm not really concerned with what you, or all of you, believe. I can visualize a day when Baptists might stop believing and preaching the Bible. If and when that happens in my lifetime, I won't even want your ordination paper. What I will do, and intend to do, is preach the Bible."

There was a brief, stunned quiet, then I heard Brother Trueblood invite Preacher to have a seat. Then he began to pour oil on the ruffled water. He was pretty good, and I think even Preacher and Brother Dacus forgot the original question. But I found I was pressed up against the door, listening.

Well, they got back on safe ground, and the rest of the questions were about where Cain got his wife, did the rapture happen before or after the tribulation, did he have a copy of the Revised Standard Version, and such like. While they were motioning and seconding, I ducked out the back, joined Wes at the front, and we walked over to the church. Wes said, "Air you all right, Ollie? You look a little pale around the gills."

I told him we almost lost Preacher, and that I'd explain later, but to give me a drag on his cigarette butt before we got to the church door.

After a notable sermon on Communism by Brother Trueblood, the ordaining council had Preacher and Sister Sara come up front. Then everybody on the council and the deacons went by to lay hands on Preacher, seeing who could whisper the most memorable prayer, or word of wisdom, so that others could hear it without it sounding intentional.

I was behind Brother Dacus, and heard him whisper in Preacher's ear, "I'm going to keep my eye on you, young man!"

Me, I whispered, "Preacher, your hackles are still up, but I believe your hair is laying down a little better on top." Sara looked real proud, but I could tell she wished she could lay a hand on top of his head and push his hair back down where it belonged.

Barber shops aren't open on Mondays, but early Tuesday morning, Sister Sara drove Preacher to Clarksville, and sat in the car while Preacher's last chance for respectability was scattered on the floor by Bob the barber's clippers.

12

ORDINANCE OF WATER

Preaching must be a little bit like baseball—it don't hurt to do a little scouting to improve your game. When Piney Creek Church, one of the oldest churches in the state, brought in old Leather-lungs McLean to lead a revival, Preacher was curious to go—especially after he heard the revival had gone on for three straight weeks with no sign of the Lord (or Leather-lungs) letting up.

I tried to explain that we folks from Blacksburg didn't frequent the Flat Rock area, and that folks ought to keep to their own side of the creek, but he was bound and determined to go. So, on Saturday, when I had to go down that way to get to London to pick up a round stone table top for Millard, Preacher said he wanted to ride with me.

Coming back, Preacher looked out the window on his side, saw a sign in front of the Piney Church, and read it for my benefit as we passed. "Revival—Third Week. Brother Latham McLean, Evangelist." That didn't impress me none. I'd heard of old Leather-lungs before, when he was preaching up at Hickeytown. And the revival's duration didn't impress me, neither. I told Preacher that it was old Leather-lungs's modus operandi—a good revival was a cash cow, and he believed in stripping the teats.

But I could see that it was eating on Preacher. He just couldn't imagine preaching every night for weeks on end, and still have a crowd. He wanted to go and hear this voice crying in the wilderness for himself. I thought I had him cooled down till we got back to town, and we stopped at Dolph's store to pick up the mail. Someone said they'd heard they had a hundred and thirty-seven people saved so far at the Piney Church revival, and the meeting was going into a fourth, and maybe a fifth week, according to the Lord's leading.

I knew that song, "the Lord's leading." It meant there was still milk in those udders. But it just fanned Preacher's fire—he had to go.

So we went. Now, you have to know that the church at Piney, which is out by Flat Rock, is a bit different. Only the women and kids sit inside. All the men stay outside in the dark, leaning on car fenders, or hunkering on the ground, listening to the singing and preaching through the open windows. That's real convenient, 'cause when they get under conviction, they can get reinforcement from a bottle or jug. When we got there, I started looking for a place to hunker, but Preacher said, "Come on, we're going inside." I didn't want to start an argument with a preacher in front of those Flat Rockers and Piney folks, so I followed him in. There we were, the only men, except for Leather-lungs, in the middle of a crowd of women and children. I thought I could hear some cackling from the yard, but it was soon drowned out by the singing.

After working our way through the songbook, they took up the offering in a Tucker lard bucket. It didn't take long, so I figured the udders were about dry after all. I looked up at Leather-lungs, saw a frown on his face, and knew it was so. Maybe Preacher and I were the only ones who gave. Preacher pulled out his wallet and fished around for a small bill. I was more prepared; I had a folded-up dollar bill in my pocket so the folks couldn't see whether it was a one or what.

It startled us both when old Leather-lungs called Preacher up to the rostrum to lead a prayer of thanksgiving for the offering. I don't know if he recognized Preacher as a preacher, or if he would have picked either one of us, since we were the only men in the place. Preacher warn't prepared, of course, so he prayed too long. By that I mean that while he was praying, old Leather-lungs soft-footed off the rostrum, out the side door, and slipped through the pine grove and was gone. Once the revival had wound down, there warn't much left to do but the baptizing, and he must've not been much on baptizing.

Well, guess who got to preach the revival that night? Preacher. There was a whole church (and parking pasture) full of folks, and somebody had to do something. I guess he was pretty mad at being snookered into a position like that, but he got his feet out of the basket that night—he took it out on the crowd. He knew that when the news got back to Blacksburg that he had preached at Piney, there would be Willie Ned to pay. Annie and Wilbur and Elmo would see to that.

He made it short and sweet, and when he got wound down and gave the invitation, two men came in out of the dark, knelt down at the altar, and asked for prayer. They turned out to be Roscoe and Emmett Jenks, and they were from Blacksburg.

Well, Preacher had sense enough to close the revival with that service, but he didn't know, as heir apparent, that he had a lot of baptizing to do—a hundred and thirty-seven, plus his two. And he had yet to do his first baptizing. Fortunately, the Piney folks wanted to have their baptizing in three weeks, which was their church anniversary. That gave Preacher two Sundays to learn how, and two converts to practice on. He urged the Jenks brothers to come to church at Blacksburg the next Sunday and ask for baptism. Which they did.

As long as I can remember, Blacksburg had always baptized in Horsehead Creek, up near Hagarville. So Sunday afternoon saw most of Blacksburg headed up there to see Preacher doing his first baptizing, just like John the Baptizer, in a cold-running mountain stream.

Preacher and Roscoe waded out to deep water and was just getting set when Preacher learned his first lesson: You don't stand on "tank" methods in a running stream—when the water is moving, you move with it. It ain't too dignified leaning a man into the water and then have him take off downstream before you can retrieve him. Lesson number two came along as a bonus with lesson number one, with no time interval—you don't baptize downstream, unless you are serious about "burying in the waters." While Preacher was studying on deep sea navigation, and grappling with the problem of water displacement, his deacons were grading his papers. You see, while the Lord drops a plumb bob on His people, it's the deacons who throw a framing square on the preachers. While Preacher was trying to rescue Roscoe without any leverage, and at the same time repeat his scriptural formula in a cold river, his deacons were taking notes.

Then it was Emmett's turn, and Preacher, shaken by his near disaster with Roscoe, corrected his earlier mistakes, and dipped Emmett so quick he didn't have time to close his mouth. Preacher looked pleased with himself, until Wilbur came flogging down to the bank, hollering, "Preacher, you have to do that one over! You didn't get him all the way under—I saw his elbow, and it didn't even get wet. Mark my word, he ain't baptized, not according to the Scripture, and I bet he won't stick it out a month."

Preacher just stood there with the cold water working up a little steam around him, embarrassed in front of his flock, not knowing whether to snorkel or pray. He prayed, and for quite a long time, too. Reckon he would have prayed longer, till the people forgot about Emmett's elbow, recognizing of course that Wilbur warn't going to forget, but about that time he got a cramp in his leg and reached out to grab hold of Wilbur for support. And wouldn't you know it, he pulled Wilbur in, and Wilbur went under.

Well, Wilbur didn't take offense, allowing as how it was an accident—but he vowed never to get that close to Preacher in a creek again. But from that day on, he watched Emmett right close, looking for that malodorous pagan elbow to spread till it recaptured the rest of his body. Let Emmett try working on a Sunday, or leave a beer can in the back of his pickup, and Wilbur would get on his case so quick it would've made your heart ache to see his loyalty to the gospel purity of the church.

Preacher had one more Sunday before he was due to go to the Piney baptizing, and he needed more experience. During the Sunday night service, Sally Peete got saved, so Preacher set her baptism for the next Sunday. This time, though, he set it up to be at Slim's stock pond. Since said stock pond was right in town, everybody including the Methodists and Church of Christers came. It was going to be a good challenge for Preacher, since he had a flair for the unexpected: Sally weighed in at about three or four feed sacks, and that's about how many it took to make her a dress.

Preacher didn't know her, so he asked me as we walked down to the stock pond if I thought she was excitable, or given to shouting, or anything like that. I told him I thought he could rely on her staying in the water, unless she stepped on a snake, in which case I hoped he could carry her out, because she would be climbing up on his shoulders for sure. I guess that shook him up some, because his eyes kept roving the bank as he stepped into the water. He was so intent on looking for snakes that he forgot to take off his Sunday shoes.

Well, Sally waded on out to where Preacher was, and we all gathered round to sing before he did his holy office. Along about the fifth verse, I noticed that somehow, the water was higher up on them than it had been on the first verse. Maybe they noticed that too, and Preacher hurried to get into position—but only the upper part of his body moved. I slewed my eyes over at Slim, who sang bass next to me, and he looked at me kind of mournful-like. He shook his head and said, "I tried to tell him, but he wouldn't listen. That pond has a mud bottom."

By dint of effort, Preacher got his body twisted at the waist, and started a pained intonation of "In the name of . . ." as he lowered Sally into the water. Now, Sally was more than adequately buoyant, and it was apparent that Preacher didn't have enough leverage to get her underwater. We tried to add a little body English from the seashore, and it must have helped, because he finally got her immersed. But then he couldn't lift her. Wilbur, standing safely way back on the bank, said in a loud stage whisper, "Why in tarnation don't he have the gumption to get in position?" Nobody heard him, though, because Sally was thrashing around, trying to get above water.

Finally, Preacher got himself squared around, but only after he jerked his feet right out of them Sunday shoes, which was stuck deep in the clay mud bottom of Slim's pond. But getting free long enough to help Sally, who was already doing her best to make a solo exit from the water, was only a temporary solution. Sally was blubbering but breathing air again, but they still weren't making any progress towards coming out. Preacher knew he was supposed to pray after baptizing, but he just looked over at me, as big-eyed as Wes. Elmo glared like he wanted to leave Preacher in the gumbo, but Wilbur said, "Get that fool out of there."

It took four of us—we took off our shoes first—to get them out of the mud. I helped Preacher, and the other three hauled Sally loose. The sucking sounds of them coming out of the mud were so vulgar that Sister Sara started singing "Victory In Jesus" to drown out the noise, and we all joined in.

After that, until we finally installed a real baptistry behind the rostrum, whenever we had another convert, Slim invariably spoke up in church and asked, "Where are we going to have the baptizing?" We never got a chance to vote on it—Preacher would always announce that we would be going to Horsehead Creek. That vexed Wilbur: He would mutter on for weeks about us being a democratic body, and losing our Baptist distinctives.

About the only thing really lost, though, was a pair of Sunday shoes. I offered to help Preacher retrieve them after we finished with Sally, but he said, "No, I think I'll go barefoot. It was good enough for the Apostle Paul, and it ought to be good enough for me."

As we walked back to the church, I whispered to myself, "Well, Piney, here we come, ready or not."

13

JONAH

The next Saturday, Wes and I hitched a ride with Buford to the county sale. Coming home, we got off at the Conoco station along about the shank of the evening, said, "Much obliged" to Buford, and started walking the rest of the way home. Our route went by the parsonage, so we naturally looked over that way to see if Preacher was home, getting ready for the Piney marathon. The parsonage sets in a narrow vee lot, so we passed the back porch first, and could see something going on through the screen. Up and down . . . up and down.

Wes and I slowed, looked at each other, and came to a dead stop to watch. It was pretty obvious even to our feeble minds that Preacher was practicing baptizing: up and down . . . up and down. We decided to count. We got up to fifty-one, when Wes said, "This is ridiculous. He's going to wear himself out."

"Wes, he's just seeing how many times he can bend over," I said. "If he can't handle a hundred and thirty-seven bundles of air, then he sure can't handle that many real bodies. And who knows, there may be some more Sally Peetes waiting for him. Let's get on home before I start leaning with him."

I thought church at Blacksburg would be pretty tame the next morning, with a big event like the Piney baptizing crouched in the afternoon. But I forgot about Annie and Wilbur and Elmo. After Sunday School, Preacher came in from the side room where he had been teaching a class, and they were all three sitting together on the front pew, ready for church to start. Or, more correctly, they were ready to *start* church. We had seen them sitting together before, but not too often—just when they were getting ready to fire a preacher. Wes and I were sitting at the back as usual, and I could tell from looking at the back of Elmo's and Wilbur's necks that they were stiff. Annie's hair jiggled every little bit, so I knew she was rehearsing what she was going to say.

Dolph started the song service, and when it and the offering were over, Sister Sara stood up to sing a special number, which in good Baptist tradition consists of the first, second, and last verses. The song was "Tell It Again," and as she was singing, she noticed the adamantine trio on the front row, and decided to sing all seven of the verses.

Sara sat down, winded, but before Preacher could get up to preach, Aunt Annie rose and said, "I want to say a few words." That would have been a first for Annie, but I guess the word "few" is relative. Anyway, she reviewed what had been happening down at Piney, how unfitting it was for our preacher to be seen down there, and what's more, he didn't have no right to go traipsing off down there to baptize that riff-raff, and if he did, getting bit by a snake would serve him right. I gave momentary consideration to the odds of being snakebit in a herd of at least two hundred and seventy-six legs, and thought he'd be safe—at least, a lot safer than here.

Then Elmo got up and allowed as how if Preacher baptized them folks, the next thing we knew, some of them would be wanting to come and join Blacksburg Baptist Church, and wouldn't that be a fine kettle of fish! Then Wilbur got up and said he was worried about us losing our Baptist distinctives, because Preacher hadn't asked permission to preach at Piney, nor baptize there neither. By that, he meant that Preacher hadn't asked the deacons. Then he said that he was making a motion to have a called business meeting right after the service, but he didn't get a second.

I was watching to see how Preacher was taking all of this, and saw that his lip curled a bit, then he rubbed his face as if he could wipe off all his irritation. By the time Annie finished her reprise, he was turning in his Bible, looking for some verse or other.

Preacher got up, looked over us folks like he was getting ready to hold a mass funeral, and started reading from the Acts of the Apostles. The sermon was about the Apostle Peter being chinchy about going down to this Gentile house on the seashore to baptize the new converts at Cornelius's house. He also reached back into the Old Testament, and painted a pretty clear picture of Jonah whining around about the riff-raff of Nineveh being allowed to enjoy the forgiveness of God. Then he started pulling in some story about a New Testament rascal who had just got out from under some astronomical debt, and wouldn't forgive some guy who owed him two bits.

I liked it when Preacher preached from the underneath side of a curled lip, and I think most everybody else did, too . . . except maybe the targets. Elmo jumped up and said, "All right, Preacher, that's enough! Go ahead and do your baptizing, but don't expect me to be there to pull you out of the mud." Annie twisted in her seat like she was trying to bore a hole in the wood, then popped up, flounced down the aisle, and declared, "Come on, Wes, we're going home!" That left Wilbur, who said plaintively, "Preacher, we've just got to do things democratically around here or we are going to lose our New Testament distinctives." With that, things sort of fizzled, the service drifted on to conclusion, and we all went home.

Well, Preacher had already learned not to eat before funerals, and I expect he didn't eat much before he went to Piney that afternoon, neither. Quite a few folks from Blacksburg went, but they all, except Sister Sara, stood on the west bank of the creek and watched. Preacher looked over at us from the Piney side with practically the whole populations of Flat Rock and Piney gathered around him. Before he started down into the water, he looked our way again, shook his head, and turned to the waiting line. I shivered; somehow it felt like the Last Judgment, and I warn't sure anymore which side of the creek had the sheep, and which, the goats.

Flat Rock gets its name, as you may know, from the horizontal ledges of sandstone that stairstep down the creekbank on the Piney side. Anyone from around here has memorized from the low water times where each level is, and makes use of that knowledge when fishing the area. The kids know where the ledges are for a different reason—when you want to dive in for a nice summertime swim, you don't want to come up with a permanent knot on your head. Of course, Preacher didn't know about any of them, so it was only a matter of time.

First, Preacher announced that due to the great number, he would like for the candidates for baptism to enter the water in groups of twenty at a time, holding each others' hands, in a semicircle. After the crowd of one hundred and thirty-seven had gathered into groups, Preacher prayed. I bowed my head, but parted my eyebrows so I could keep a watchful eye on things: I had no intention of swimming across to look for a disappeared Preacher when he stepped off into deep water—it was too far from the west bank. Besides, the Piney folks were acting friendly, so they surely wouldn't let a man of God drown before their very eyes. Wes whispered a comforting thought to me right after the Amen: "Can Preacher swim?"

The first ragged semicircle of baptizees entered the water, and Preacher began. He was about fourteen feet from the Piney bank, where the water was about three and a half feet deep. I recognized the rock he was on, though he couldn't see it in the turgid water. The first group of twenty went fairly smoothly, even with two of the older ladies coming out of the water shouting and throwing water all the way back to the bank, and one middle-aged man who wanted to give his testimony before being dipped.

The second group contained a large family that had been split in two by the groupings of twenty. When Preacher got them finished and it was time for the third group, all the family members who had just been baptized wanted to stay in the water while the rest of their kin were immersed. Piney Creek was getting a little crowded. I heard Preacher say, "Wait a minute, folks, let's all move out in the water a bit more to make room for everybody. This water here is a little too shallow, anyway." He beckoned with his arms while he backed up farther into the creek. I think he was saying something else when he disappeared.

Sara screamed, and everybody on that side that warn't already in the water got there in a hurry. It reminded me of a school of hickory shad swimming for their lives at the approach of a big bass. All of us on the west side were at the water's edge, shouting advice, and peeling our eyes for a sign of our Jonah. The McAnelly twins saw him first, downstream a bit, crawling up on a ledge where he could stand in two feet of water.

I heard someone from our bank holler, "Hey, Preacher, it ain't deep enough there, air it?" I turned around to see who it was, and high up on the bank behind us stood Elmo, grinning and slapping his leg to beat the band.

Well, when the long afternoon was over, and all souls were accounted for, most of them wet, Wes and I rode back with Preacher and Sister Sara. After awhile, I said, "Preacher, you're always talking about going to the mission field in South America. Isn't that where they have those peeranha fish that eat the flesh off your bones before you can wade out of a river? How in the world do they baptize down there?"

Things were silent in the front seat for a few minutes, but then Preacher answered, "No problem, Ollie. Down there, the deacons do the baptizing."

GERALD EUGENE NATHAN STONE

66

14

FURNITURE

Our church is infected with a lot of memories. Everything in the church building has a sacred history, and all you have to do is touch something with an unsanctified hand and you will be inducted into the Order of Uzzah.

It probably got started with the pulpit, the one that George W. Truett preached from way back yonder. Preacher didn't know that, of course, when he moved the pulpit one Sunday afternoon so he could use an easel on the rostrum that night. He found out that he had entered into the Holy of Holies without washing his hands and feet. The lady Levite who guarded the Holy Place was—you guessed it, Aunt Annie. She ruffled her feathers and rumbled like a hen when a varmint is threatening to steal her chicks. She flogged right up to Preacher, and demanded, "*Who* moved that pulpit?"

Well, Preacher looked at her, then at the pulpit, and supposing his transgression was having knocked the lace doily to the floor, he picked it up and patted it into place on top of the pulpit. He said, "I did, Sister Annie. It sure is rickety. We ought to get a new one from Booneville, especially if we are going to buy new pews."

"Young man, you put that pulpit right back where it came from. George W. Truett once preached from that sacred desk, and it's going to stay right where it's been all these years since."

Well, after those comments about the pulpit, Preacher should have gotten the lay of the land, but no, he waded right into that postponed war between the Sunday School and the Baptist Young People's Union that had got a former preacher run off. You see, every Baptist church that had electric lights, Delco, or lanterns had BYPU, but the movement was puny. Through the years, the puzzled leaders had whipped that mule every which way, but it just wouldn't work in a double-tree with Sunday School. On Sunday mornings in Blacksburg, Sunday School Opening Assembly was held on the north side of the church, with the piano and a lectern nearby, so the Superintendent could give his devotional thought, and also lead the opening song in close concert with the pianist. Then on Sunday night, across the aisle to the south, the BYPU Director would give his devotional thought, again with the piano and lectern nearby, so he could have close concert with the pianist.

No, we didn't have two pianos. Nobody even thought of that solution. What happened was that our one and only, poor old piano got rolled from the north side to the south side every Sunday. Every Sunday morning, the Sunday School Superintendent would drag it across to the north side. Every Sunday evening, the BYPU Director would drag it to the south side. It would have been an act of common courtesy to move the piano back when you got through with it, so that it would be at the right place for the next engagement, but what happened was, each of the aggrieved parties would declare, "If they don't move it back for me, I sure ain't going to move it for them."

Well, if you can't pet a rattlesnake, pet a copperhead—Preacher had the bright idea to have the piano put up on the rostrum, where the song leader would have better eye contact with the pianist while leading the choir. That way the piano could stay put and not wear out the floorboards going back and forth every week. I turned down Preacher's gracious offer to help him move the piano up on stage. I told him I thought he ought to wait a bit, and talk to Annie, or Elmo. He was getting to where he kind of trusted my judgment about things, so he agreed to wait.

Then, one Sunday morning, the Sunday School Superintendent showed up early, collar already hot with anticipation, and sure enough, there was the piano on the wrong side again. It was close to Sunday School time, and this being Thanksgiving Sunday, there would be a big crowd, so he hurried to move the piano back where it belonged. Wes was outside, and had intended to come in, but he was tired of getting roped into helping move that blamed piano every week, so he hung back and saw the whole scene through the side window.

The Superintendent moved the stool first. It was one of those round-topped adjustable jobs with glass-ball-and-iron-claw feet. He didn't notice that someone had run the seat out of its threads, so when he picked it up, the bottom part fell and an iron claw banged him on the big toe with a solid glass ball. He roared, threw the seat up on the rostrum, hopped over to the front pew, and sat there nursing his foot and his choler.

Then he got up and limped over to the stool, reassembled it, and placed it respectfully in position, over on the north side. Then he went back to move the piano across No-Man's-Land. He pushed, grunted a little, but it didn't move. He laid his shoulder into it, then got on the other side and pulled, then tried to rock it a little from side to side, then tried to push it again. He quit before he wore himself out, and bent down to see what was keeping the piano from rolling. He snapped upright, and banged the keyboard with a mighty fist. Someone—likely the usual suspects, Loren and Zane McAnelly— had taken the casters off.

We didn't have a devotional that morning.

I think I used the word "infected." It warn't just the holy furniture in the Tabernacle itself, but it included the Outer Court as well—in this case, the parsonage. When Preacher and Sister Sara moved in, I don't recollect that they had a single stick of furniture, so what they ended up with was a miscellaneous hodgepodge from all the people roundabouts. You probably don't realize how uncomfortable that can make living. Can you imagine having a church member come by one day, and you haven't dusted that priceless heirloom hatstand that once belonged to her Aunt Sadie? Or having someone else come by and discover that you put their three-and-a-half-legged table out on the back porch, instead of in a place of honor in the front room where everybody can see it? Or frown at you in your own house when you put your feet on their former footstool without pulling off your shoes?

Well, someone had left (I won't say "given") this wooden rocker at the parsonage. It was shaped like a renovated electrocution instrument from Tucker Penitentiary, with ruptured springs, alligatored varnish finish, and a split arm that had been wired together with baling wire. However, I think Preacher halfway liked it, since it was the only rocking chair they had, and I often saw him rocking in it. But then again, maybe it was his modern-day hair shirt, because some of his less memorable sermons were prepared sitting in that chair.

One day, Brother Eben Dothan came by, collecting stuff for a family who had been burned out across the River in Carden's Bottom. Preacher sighed, and gave up the rocker. Brother Eben loaded it with the rest of his booty, and hauled it forty-seven miles to the other end of the Dardanelle-Russellville Association, and gave it to that destitute family. Coincidentally, Preacher's sermons improved right after that.

It must have been several months later that Elmo came over to the parsonage between Sunday School and Church to use the bathroom.

Since everybody was over at the church, I guess he looked around a little. Anyways, he didn't find that rocking chair; as it turned out, it was the chair he had been rocked in as a baby, which had been brought up the River by a long-ago generation. He didn't ask Preacher before the service, and knowing Elmo, I'm surprised he didn't put his query between Point Two and Point Three of the sermon. He waited until afterward, when Preacher was back shaking hands at the door, and everybody was crowded around.

"Brother Marshall, what have you done with *my* rocking chair?" he asked bluntly. Well, charity was no excuse. Elmo wanted his rocking chair back—then and there. Preacher, shaken, asked me to go with him.

We got an early start Monday morning, and took off for Brother Eben's place, out from Russellville. We arrived to find no one at home, so we drove on to Dardanelle, and asked the pastor there who it was that had gotten burned out several months ago. Armed with that information, we struck out for the boonies. Finding someone in Carden's Bottom is not a real joy, particularly when you get close to the River, and the end of the road—if you don't belong there, everyone thinks you're a Revenue agent. One place we stopped to ask for directions, the wife said her old man had run as soon as he saw us, and was hidden below the bank leading down to the water. He didn't know nothing.

Well, we finally found the family, but we didn't find the rocker. They hadn't liked it, and had given it away to someone else. Preacher was turning into a basket case. He said, "Ollie, whatever am I going to do?" But even though I'd made mistakes similar to this, I had absolutely no encouragement to give him—it looked like Elmo would soon be moving for another Called Business Meeting.

When we got back on the county road, we stopped at the first farmhouse to draw some water for the radiator, and asked the lady of the house if anyone there had ever seen a rocker of a certain description. Preacher almost fell in the well when she told us it was down in the barn in the corn crib.

Preacher ended up paying seven dollars for that useless junk, but he seemed happy. He kept singing snatches of "The Ninety and Nine" all the way home. We had to stop once, because Preacher had got so excited, he forgot to put the radiator cap back on and we boiled dry. I let him walk to the nearest house to get some water, and I got the rocking chair out and pulled it under a shade tree on the other side of the bar ditch, and whiled away an hour. That hour proved to me that I should have gone after the water and let Preacher sit in the rocker—and that Elmo deserved to have it back.

I asked Preacher on the way home what he was going to do about the "other piece of furniture," meaning the piano, which had been stranded on the south side of the church since before Thanksgiving. He answered, "Ollie, where do you think Noah's Ark is today?" I allowed as how it was probably wherever it came to rest on the Ararat mountain, because there probably warn't two different factions shoving it from the north side to the south and back every Sabbath since the receding of the waters. "In other words," he mused, "it's right where the Lord intended it to be."

I rolled my eyes and cautioned him about taking sides in the Sunday School/BYPU feud, lessen he wanted Elmo and Wilbur and Annie to recommend him for our ex-preachers' club. He was quick to remind me that the Lord's works are often mysterious, but always with our best interests at heart, whether we know it or not.

When we rolled up to the parsonage, there was a big black DeSoto with a Little Rock license tag in the driveway. After unloading the rocking chair where Elmo would be sure to see it, we went inside to get a drink of water. There Sister Sara introduced the visitor—Miss Sue Ellen Pruitt, a WMU bigwig from the Baptist headquarters in

Little Rock, who also happened to be Sara's second cousin on her father's side. She said, "The truck should be here pretty soon. He stopped to gas up at the Conoco station on the highway. When he gets here, maybe these two gentlemen will help him unload."

I hadn't ever heard Preacher, or any preacher for that matter, called a gentleman, and I hadn't any memory of it applying to me, neither, but I stood a little straighter, anyway. I thought, "Sister Sara's finally got tired of all these hand-me-downs, and this relation of hers is giving her some decent furniture."

About then, the truck drove up, but kept right on going across the road and stopped in front of the church. We walked over, opened the rear doors of the truck, and stared at a used but nicely kept Hamilton electronic organ. It was a gift from Miss Pruitt to our church, in honor of Sara and her husband.

I looked at Preacher suspiciously, thinking he must have known about this all the time. But no, he was in a state of shock, which soon gave way to joy—it was the answer to our piano dilemma. The organ could go on one side and the piano on the other, and there would be music on both sides of the church.

After depositing our burden, the truck driver and I went outside to roll a smoke. Preacher said he would lock up, but when he didn't come out right away, I flipped my cigarette and went back to the door. He was on his knees by the organ, thanking the Lord for the gift, I guessed. Then he got on down on his hands and looked under it, checking to see whether it had casters.

15

WATERS OF SILOAM

Sometimes Preacher did the best job of being a pastor when he didn't know he was doing it.

Old man Stonaker and his wife had moved to Blacksburg to retire some years before Preacher arrived. Nobody knew why he picked our town. But being as how he lived a couple of doors down from the parsonage, and across the street from Wilbur, Preacher put him on his prospect list. That's one of the few honors we had around here, getting on a prospect list. Only thing was, old man Stonaker was developing a prospect list of his own, and Preacher was on it.

Probably every person in this world has a nemesis that dogs his path. The sinner sees a saint smiling through the twisted face of crippling disease, and loses sleep trying to figure it out; the saint sees the sinner enjoying his life of sin and loses sleep wondering how good it feels. The trouble with Stonaker was he already had more beliefs than he needed, including religious beliefs, but he was flat out of contentment. According to Millard, who sorted the mail, he subscribed to every radical and near-radical magazine and paper there was. Millard also saw an awful lot of correspondence with Hoxsey, Mayo, Guadalajara, Rochester, M. D. Anderson, and a bunch of other cancer clinics.

The trouble with Preacher was he didn't know Stonaker had been in and out of most of these, and had come to Blacksburg to die.

Well, Preacher didn't have nothing in mind but sharing the plain old gospel, but Stonaker, now, he had something fancy that threw Preacher into confusion at every visit. Preacher was young and hadn't developed much of a nose for sniffing out cold trails, so there he'd sit with old man Stonaker, chasing some esoteric doctrine of mind control or Egyptology, getting nowhere close to brass tacks. And all the while, that old man was just sitting there aching for Preacher to break through all that intellectual, pagan hooey and see him for what he really was—a sick and shriveled-up shuck of a man with a healthy boarder inside, arguing over who had rights to the premises.

I guess Millard came the closest to seeing the solution when he said that all Preacher needed was just to lose his patience. But Preacher, like the rest of us, kept close tabs on people and situations that didn't matter, and overlooked people and situations that did matter. Anyhow, their ongoing set-to over theology soon got sidetracked by the Almighty. Maybe even He gets tired of people forever studying and palavering about how His name is spelled, or how to explain that God could be one but also three, and just wants somebody to pay attention to what He is trying to say. Sometimes, though, He has to whomp you up alongside the head to get your attention.

Stonaker's neighbor, old Miz Emmer, was sitting in the swing one day, listening to Preacher and Stonaker across the fence having a go at evolution, but whether she knew what they were saying, we never knew. At any rate, she hadn't said ten words to anyone in as many years. Walter was tinkering on his brother Wilbur's car across the road, when she up and gave this quavery little yell, and keeled over. 'Course, Preacher and Walter raced over, but she was gone—probably dead before she hit the porch.

Then, before they could get the news down at the post office, one of the McAnelly twins came loping through the yard, yelling that something bad had happened down in the Bend. About that same time, Jeff Bledsoe's truck came hurtling around the corner, horn going, and karrumphed north across the tracks headed for Clarksville. Preacher ran down to the parsonage to use the phone to call for some help, and got Sister Sara to go over to Miz Emmer's to see what she could do while he took out after Jeff. We all found out shortly enough that what had happened down in the Bend was that Dub Wheeler had contributed his leg to the hay baler. Somewhere in Arkansas, a vegetarian cow was going to have a surprise for breakfast.

By the time Preacher got back to Miz Emmer's, the Goin Home folks had just left for Clarksville with her body. There stood old man Stonaker, just on the other side of the fence, not having moved since the first domino fell, a copy of *Plain Truth* dangling from one hand, and a *Rosicrucian Digest* from the other. He watched Preacher mother-henning around Miz Emmer's brother and sister-in-law until they went back in the house to gather some things to take to the funeral home.

Walter was still standing on Miz Emmer's porch when Preacher moseyed over to the fence and said, sort of innocent-like, "You know, Miz Emmer, she never knew what hit her, and that's a blessing. She knew the Lord, though, and I know she's already in His presence. So many people linger and die a slow death with cancer or some other terrible disease, without being saved, and that's such a sad thing." Walter said he saw old Stonaker drop his papers, grip that hogwire fence hard, and almost shake it out of the ground.

Preacher wouldn't have made much of a bird dog, but I guess when a bobwhite is fluttering so close in front of your nose that you have to close your eyes to keep the feathers out, then it ain't too hard to point. At any rate, Stonaker and Preacher started having weekly meetings where they talked about the Bible. Millard said the old man just started tossing his magazines in the trash can at the post office, without even tearing off the brown paper to look at the covers. It warn't long before Preacher had baptized the old man in Horsehead Creek, but they still had some lively discussions that Preacher called his "seminary extension course in alternative religions."

16

WAKE

Some of the old ways were better; not all of them, but some. Even Preacher had to admit that.

We were sitting around Dolph's store, guiding the shade from one side to the other, led by old Spot, Wilbur's dog. That dog marked the seasons by how he lay in the shade. Some people talk about Ground-hog Day, but around here, nobody even knows what a groundhog looks like—maybe Spot killed them out and took their place. Anyway, that dog, as winter turned to spring, liked to lay in the sunshine, but as the season moved on, he liked to lay on the recently-sunned earth, but actually in the shade. Then, when it got good and hot in the summer, he would lay in the shade, on the part that hadn't felt sunshine since yesterday. When fall came, he would lay in the shade, but on the part that was most recently in the sun. In winter, he was like us old codgers—he moved inside to the potbelly stove.

We were discussing whether it was about time for Spot to change to the next phase of comfort, when Preacher drove up and asked me to go with him down to the Bend. Dub Wheeler had up and died from an infection in his stub of a leg where he had got caught in the hay baler; Preacher said his family wanted to have a wake at the home, and he didn't know what that meant.

I told him on the way down to Dub's place that a wake was just sitting up for the dead. Everybody seemed to agree that it was proper to wash, dress, and lay the dead out on a sheet-covered set of planks in the home, though most were using caskets now. The body was supposed to lie by an open window, with a lighted lamp on a side table, and one chair where the watcher could sit for awhile, study the dead, read the Bible, or meditate on the brevity of life. And, of course, keep an eye on the window curtains and the lamp wick, in case there was any sign of the spirit still hanging around.

Preacher started trying to straighten me out on that, but we had arrived before he had much chance. I did tell him as we got out of the car that the family probably didn't need to be educated on those fine points right now, so he sort of simmered down. It was already towards the shank of the evening, so we took supper with the family, and then sat around on the front porch talking. Pretty soon, folks started drifting in—neighbors who had gone home to milk, and late-arriving family members.

The women folks went on in the house to comfort the widow and kids; the men folks gathered in the front yard under the cedar trees, and smoked and swapped quiet talk. Eventually, Preacher and I went in to stand by the bier for a while. I noticed that the curtains were still, and the lamp warn't flickering, but Dub's old blue-tick hound under the house was putting out a mournful howling, so I kept my eyes on events. Dub had on a black suit, which was something of a shock, since I had never seen him in anything but overalls, even in church.

Preacher whispered to me, "How come there aren't any flowers?" I told him that Dub was not a woman—only women got flowers, and then not always. Usually if they did, it was only a spray placed in the hands of the deceased.

We didn't stay all night, since Preacher needed to get back to town, so he could get ready for the funeral service the next day. That was just as well, because the men folks were getting a little noisy out under the trees—I heard the sound of removed stoppers several times, and noticed that all the young boys had been shooed into the house.

Next day was different. They had Dub's coffin surrounded with flowers, both cut and potted. Most of Dub's folks by his first marriage lived in California, where they do things a little peculiar, and it looked like they had cleaned out the Clarksville florist. The folks from the Goin Home had stacked them everywhere, including around the George W. Truett pulpit. Since I was a pallbearer, I had a front row seat, and looking up through the Garden of Eden, I could just barely see Preacher between some gladiolus and mums.

After the music was over, Preacher got up, approached the pulpit, parted the flowers and ferns, looked out over the congregation and down at the coffin, and began to preach. Occasionally, he would shift his Bible to the other hand, and move another piece of flora. He looked sort of like a frog in Aunt Annie's flowerbed. About that time, he sneezed, and I noticed that his eyes were swelling up. For a minute, I thought it was from grief, but he didn't really know the deceased, and had already gotten the obituary wrong. Besides, he'd quit grieving so much at funerals after that business with the little old lady from Horsehead Lake.

No, this was hay fever, pure and simple. I never saw anyone puff up so, and so fast. We practically had to lead him off the rostrum so he could precede the casket down the aisle to the front door. He wandered to the left, then to the right, like old Rupert Haseltine on a Saturday night bender, then he stumbled and fell right smack into the Widow Wheeler's lap. She had been as dry-eyed as a Mode O'Day mannequin until Preacher landed on her, with his eyes squirting tears and his nose dribbling down on his lip. The startled widow then began to bawl, and wrapped Preacher in her arms, pressing his face to her ample bosom.

Not sure what to do, Preacher remembered what Brother Crossnoes had done in a difficult situation, so he began to pray out loud. This only intensified Widow Wheeler's hold, so Preacher started saying, "Amen! Amen!" over and over, and slipped to his knees in the aisle to see if that would extricate him from the clutches of her grief.

Sister Sara was in the choir loft, and had a good ringside seat. She wrinkled her brow, bit her lip a little, then leaned over the rail to whisper to Miss Kinnamon at the piano. I later heard an embroidered version of what she said—something like, "Play something loud, damn it, before he has to marry her!" At any rate, the pianist did look shocked, and came down on the keyboard *presto* and *fortissimo*. I'd never heard that tune, but it served its purpose—everybody, including Preacher and the Widow Wheeler, stood bolt upright. Preacher wobbled off down the aisle, hoping that the hearse hadn't gone off and left him. I think he was about ready to jump into Dub's grave and pull it in after him.

Well, lots of little conversations sprang up in the graveside crowd. Miz Clendenning, who was something of a wag, said, "I'll pay extra for that kind of service when my husband dies." A couple of the deacons were looking at one another, shaking their heads. But Wes and I couldn't say nothing—we just stood there, shivering a little, with tears running down our cheeks. You might have thought we were grieving for poor old Dub, but in fact, we were doing our doggonedest not to bust out laughing.

Widow Wheeler showed up several times for "grief counseling." She was having problems handling her loss. Sister Sara made it a point to be there each time she came to see Preacher, to help ease her pain.

Anyhow, Preacher finally agreed with me, saying he thought he would like funerals better without flowers, except maybe those planted on the grave afterward.

17

PROSELYTIZING

It may be true that opposites attract, but you couldn't prove it by Rat and Ethyl. Those two were so much alike, they got confused about which public toilet to go to. I could say, "Did you see Rat?" or I could say, "Did you see Ethyl?" But there warn't any need to say both. If you didn't see one, you sure didn't see the other. They were one peculiar couple of beings, but I tell you, if I had just lost my best friend, they were who I'd like to meet coming home from the cemetery. Nothing like Rat or Ethyl, or Rat *and* Ethyl, as I was redundantly saying, to cheer one up.

I was keeping the cash register for Oran one time down at the Conoco cafe, and Preacher was standing there selecting a toothpick while paying up. Rat and Ethyl were sharing one of Oran's Seven for a Dollar hamburger specials, and Preacher was passing the time with them. Like always, they were both in overalls, with sockless brogans, and limp straw hats drooping around their hairy ears. Neither of them had any teeth, but they both had an aura of affability that would have charmed a wet hen into being hustled off her nest.

I saw Preacher reading this Conoco ad taped to the front of the cash register, which said, "Win a Trip to Paris!" He said, "Hey, Rat, how would you all like to go to Paris?"

Rather than lay his burger (number three) down, Rat just tucked it on in for safekeeping, seemed to find it subject for thoughtful study, though whether it was the question or the hamburger, I don't know, when Ethyl up and answered, "Reckon not, honey, we ain't done the milking yet."

Preacher was still sort of new around here then, and didn't catch that hot grounder—Paris was the county seat of our neighbor county to the south, but because it was across the River, and the nearest bridge was at Russellville or Clarksville, I guess Preacher hadn't heard of it. So Rat stepped up and polished off the inning with, "Reckon we could go Saturday, iffen you've a mind to."

Preacher never did decide what happened to his toothpick. He was still looking for it when I excused myself to go air up some tires.

Well, after that, it seemed like Preacher just sort of adopted Rat and Ethyl. He came into the post office one day, looking solemn and dignified like they teach preachers to look nowadays, but not having the exact hang of it yet. I could see that he was busting inside to find a place to cackle or gossip or something, like there was a fountain inside him welling up and just dying for a place to slop over.

Seems he had been over to Rat and Ethyl's right after one of our spring showers. He knew they were Church of Christers, but they lived right down the road from Preacher and Sara, and he didn't know better. Probably thought it was just a neighborly visit, never dreaming that before the week was out, he'd have every Campbellite between the Bend and Flat Rock accusing him of "proselyting."

Anyhow, he went through the gate, which warn't there no more, navigated across the loose boards that made the front porch a booby trap, and started to knock, but the door was open so he just sort of looked in. Rat, and of course, Ethyl, were moving their bed, carrying on with each other on all the multifarious advantages of this location over that location. Preacher looked at the ceiling, which Rat and Ethyl didn't have, if you go by the pure definition of the word. Rain was dripping through holes in their worn-out shingle roof, and they were looking for a dry spot. Most folks would be upset if the roof leaked on their mattress every time it rained, but Rat or Ethyl, or Rat and Ethyl? No siree! Why, moving that bed to maximum, or minimum, vantage point was just a delightful episode, often repeated, in the lives of the most unlikely honeymooners you ever saw.

They never saw Preacher; they just chattered away at each other. Preacher said he felt like he had stumbled into a secret shrine, listening to and watching those two rustic lovebirds make moving furniture a ritual of devotion and ecstasy.

So Preacher backed out of the doorway, forgetting about the booby traps, and stepped on a Campbellite board just aching to raise up and whack a Baptist preacher in what they considered the most useful part of that profession. That was when Preacher got introduced to the domino theory. By the time he had been flayed by every loose board on that porch, upset the sow under the house, and got Old Tige after him, it took Rat twenty minutes to extricate him from what was left of the front porch. Preacher warn't hurt, but he was pretty shook up. Rat and Ethyl picked him up and laid him on their bed. He was still sort of stunned, until "ping . . . ping . . . ping" brought him back to his senses. He focused on a leak above, which had focused on him. Rat thought, and Ethyl said, "Just lay still there, Preacher, and we'll move this bed till we get you in a dry place."

They spent the next half hour rolling him from one part of that misbegotten house to another, with him too weak to move, and getting dizzier with every relocation. Finally, one caster of the bed fell through a knot hole, and everything stopped abruptly. They looked at each other for a few moments, then someone started to titter, and then they all began laughing like a bunch of school girls at a Valentine's party.

Preacher and I had a good laugh about it, and didn't give it another thought until the next Sunday evening. I was there when Wilbur brought it up at the deacons' meeting. He said he was passing by on the road, coming back from the swap meet, and saw Preacher through Rat and Ethyl's window, which warn't hard, since they didn't have any. If it warn't bad enough that he was even there, Wilbur reported he had seen the three of them bouncing around on their bed, crying, laughing, and slapping each other, carrying on like a bunch of "happy-costals."

Preacher had dodged some other bullets at the church with his baptizing and funeral preaching, but now he was before the Sanhedrin and daylight was not far off. He was startled at first, and maybe a little scared, but while they waited for him to respond to this charge of unbecoming conduct, and with Campbellites at that, all he could do was stand there, working his face. Then he busted out laughing.

By the time he had exhausted that run on the "sillies," the meeting had gotten mighty still. Wilbur was measuring him, and Elmo already had him mentally stretched and quartered.

I knowed there was only one thing to do. I wall-eyed over at Wes, and we both started laughing and slapping our legs to beat the band. Finally, Wilbur sort of gave a sick grin, but Elmo, he just made a motion to adjourn.

18

CONVERSION

It seemed like Preacher was catching it from every side, so one Friday I asked him if he wanted to take a breather and go hunt arrowheads. He turned into a boy before my very eyes. So we took off and drove down to the Bend, where he parked his car by the cemetery, and we cut off cross-country on foot to a ridge overlooking the River.

I had a pocket full of Bull Durham sacks, and Preacher had a tow sack. I told him, "Preacher, if you're serious about collecting arrowheads, you're going to have to start rolling your own so you can have little sacks like these here. Even if you find the biggest cache of relics on the River, there's no way you could carry a tow sack full."

He looked at me with big innocent eyes and said, "Oh! I thought you were going to carry them for me!"

We were finding numerous broken points, half-finished blanks, and a few good Caddo points, when the wind shifted. I stood up straight to enjoy the breeze and massage my aching back, and noticed a real ominous cloud build-up in the southwest across the River. "Preacher," I said, "if that cloud works its way in our direction, we better be ready to get off this ridge." We watched it moving, and when the water on the other side of the river started rippling, I said, "Come on, let's go." We loped downhill to the tune of rocks jiggling in our pockets, then ran across the meadow to a haystack, where we burrowed out a shelter. Just in time, too—sheets of rain started slicing across the field.

After we got our breath, Preacher said, "Ollie, one time a long time ago, five men in New England got caught in a rain like this, and crawled into a haystack to stay dry. While they were in there, they prayed. It came to be known as the Haystack Prayer Meeting, and it was the beginning of American foreign missions. Adoniram Judson and Luther Rice were two of them, and they were our first Baptist missionaries."

I knew Preacher was partial to foreign missions, so I figured that's how he knew that story. I didn't know then just how much studying he'd done on the subject, and at the moment, didn't care. When the rain quit, the air got deathly still and heavy. I crawled out of the haystack and looked around—everything was hushed and bathed in a pale yellow light. "Preacher, you better come on out. I smell trouble, and we better move fast."

"Twister?" he asked, biting his lip.

"Uh-huh, somewheres close. The Spradling place is just beyond that tree line. Maybe we can make their storm cellar." We flew over the pasture, through the tree line, jumped the fence, and hied ourselves on down the slope to Jake's place. I could see Suzie herding her kids from the house into the storm cellar as we approached. As we got closer, I could see her standing there with her mouth open, looking beyond and behind us, but I warn't interested in turning to look at what she was looking at—I wanted to see her fruit jars in that cellar.

We made it to the cellar just as the wind whipped her bonnet off and tried to tear the door out of her grip. We dove in, and I pulled

Suzie in after us, barred the door shut, and we sprawled in a heap, Preacher, kids, Suzie, and me, to catch our breath and listen. There was a mighty clap of thunder, and a long sustained crackle of lightning tearing the sky apart. I looked over at Preacher in the gloom, wondering if he was worrying about centipedes and scorpions, or about his trip down Jeannie Haseltine's cellar last year, but he was giving the kids an arrowhead each to play with. I thought, "He don't realize there's real trouble going on outside." Then there was a big roaring sound, like the freight train when it passes by Blacksburg Church on a Sunday night, and it was over.

After a few minutes, we came out of the cellar, and I looked at Widow Spradling, only I didn't know she was a widow then, but I reckon she did, or maybe she'd been one ever since she married Jake. Anyway, she stood looking toward the fields and the razorback ridge where the land drops into the flood bottom and on to the River. She shivered, pulled her shawl over her shoulders, and gathered her kids to her. "Taken," she said in a quavery voice. "I heard it when he went. Children, go in the house and get you some biscuit and onions. Ollie and Preacher and I are going for your Pa. If you please, Ollie, let's hurry. The mules aren't back, neither."

We took the slag road, the longer but quicker way to the ridge. It warn't very muddy, the storm having been one of them hop, skip, and blooey storms—long on lightning and short on rain, smelling of sulphur and mighty still.

Well, going that way, we found the last furrow where Jake and the mules had been plowing. It veered off sharp to the left, and then, like a trail of the Moabites, running straight as an arrow toward safety, right across the fresh-plowed field toward the house and storm cellar. Of course, Jake never made it. It was real queer. Not a bit of rain fell on the whole field. We saw where he shed his hat, and a little farther on his dinner bucket, whipping up those mules. You could see where the plow had bounced and bumped over the ground. Then we found the mules . . . that must have been the first loud clap of thunder we heard. They were laying on the ground, with their trace chains burned into their hide, and smoke coming off their hooves. The plow was smoking, too. Not a pretty sight at all. It made me want to up and move to Little Rock, so far away from a farm you can't remember whether roosters crow at morning or night.

The trail through the plowed field was mighty slow for us to cover after that, even though Jake's trail was pretty easy to follow. We topped the ridge, and saw the house and storm cellar dead ahead, but not a sign of Jake. I warn't paying much attention to the trail then, dreading how this day was going to end up.

But that trail pulled my eyes like a magnet. It was like follering a drunk man, first toward the house, where he probably saw his family scurrying for the cellar, and us coming over the other ridge. I guess he stopped and milled around a bit before he ran again, this time in another direction, just like a rabbit running from a dog in an open field. He'd turned almost due east and was headed for a ravine nigh the Edmonds boundary.

Widow Spradling began to cry then, but weird like, a sort of whimpering kind of crying. I couldn't stand it, so I ran ahead with Preacher right behind me, and we found Jake. We stood there looking down at him, some seven or eight feet below us in that nature-made grave without a lid, till Widow Spradling caught up. He was lying there face up, overall buckles burned to him, dead, but so help me God . . . smiling. Widow Spradling just kept clasping her bonnet and saying things like you would want to hear over your own grave.

Well, I couldn't handle it, and I'm ashamed to say it, but I whoozied down on my hands and knees and puked right there on the ridge. As soon as my head cleared, I saw Preacher kneeling down by Jake, smoothing his hair, and spreading his handkerchief over those overall buckles. Then he reached into his pocket, took out a couple of them good Caddo points, closed Jake's eyes and weighted them down with his relics. He looked up at me and said, "Ollie, can you get Suzie back to the house to stay with the kids, then go for help? I'll stay here until you can get a wagon."

I couldn't find a team that warn't spooked in the aftermath of the storm, much less a wagon. I expect Suzie had her hands full keeping the kids still and all till the women folks could get there and take charge. Rather than cut across and get Preacher's car, I took Jake's mare from the barn and beat it into town. While I was riding to the store, I remembered that I couldn't expect much help from Dolph, or Elmo, or Wilbur. They had been on the outs with Jake Spradling for many a year. Actually, there warn't any love lost between me and Jake neither, but somehow that didn't matter now.

I located Slim and he got Goin Funeral Home on the phone, and they came after the body. Preacher was still sitting there with Jake's head in his lap when they arrived. After we got him loaded up, we went by the house so the Goin Home folks could make "arrangements" with the widow, and pick up some good clothes. "Arrangements" meant they weren't sure about how much money the family could pay for their services, and figured there warn't enough for funeral home clothes.

Suzie looked scandalized at the idea of Jake being buried in a suit, and brought out a pair of clean, ironed overalls. "This will suit him just fine," she told them. "He was proud to wear them to town on Saturdays, and he'd be ashamed to be buried in anything else."

As they got ready to go, Mr. Goin asked, "You will be having the funeral in the Blacksburg church, won't you?" Suzie hesitated, looking at Preacher, who said, "Of course, where else would we be having it?"

It was getting about dark when Preacher and I got back to his car. I didn't have anything to say until we got almost into town, when I asked him how well he knew Jake. Just as I thought, he didn't know him at all. He knew Suzie and the kids well enough—they were always in church. But Jake had never been to church. Us old codgers thought he was probably an atheist, and certainly he was the meanest rascal we had ever known. I puzzled my brain a long time before I thought of a way to tell Preacher that holding a church funeral for Jake was going to cause the manure to hit the fan. I finally said, "Preacher, who are you going to get for pallbearers?"

He turned to me and said, "Ollie, I need to work on my sermons for Sunday, and the funeral is set for Monday. Would you mind taking care of that for me?"

"Preacher, I ain't never done anything like that."

"Oh, you can get Wilbur, and Dolph, and Elmo, and yourself. That makes four. Then you can ask Millard and Slim."

Oh, sure, I thought. But getting pallbearers was going to be easy compared to the problems that were waiting around the corner for Preacher.

Late Saturday night, Preacher had visitors—Elmo, Annie, and Wilbur. I had just brought by a bucket of blackberries for Sister Sara, so I was in the kitchen and heard the whole thing.

Annie, in her delightful way, said, "Preacher, you ain't going to preach that infidel Jake's funeral in our church. Not from behind our pulpit, you ain't."

Wilbur threw in his two bits about Baptist distinctives, and then Elmo said, "Preacher, how could you be meddling in the Lord's judgment? Don't you see that Jake was a great sinner before the Lord, and he had to pay? You need to come out from among them and touch not the unclean thing."

I peeked through the kitchen door, and Preacher had a thoughtful look on his face, and was scratching his chin while he surveyed these sheep with their long front teeth. He finally asked, "What is it that makes Jake Spradling so untouchable to you folks? His wife and children have been loyal to the church ever since I came."

Annie said, "That's different, 'cause they is from the Bend. That Jake Spradling was born and reared over at Flat Rock, and nothing good has ever come out of there. Besides, he was an atheist, I'm told, and can well believe it; anyone that would refuse to let his kids come to the Christmas Tree program at Blacksburg Baptist Church has got to be an atheist."

Preacher thought for another minute, and then laughed. "And I asked Ollie to get you, Wilbur, and you, Elmo, to serve as pallbearers. Sounds to me like you probably won't be available. Let's just move the funeral down to Piney Church. It's not any farther away from heaven than Blacksburg."

"Heaven!" Annie shrilled. "Jake's in hell, and you know it. No amount of preaching is going to change that. And you better not sully your ministry by going down there and try to preach him into heaven, neither."

Well, there warn't no basket for Preacher's feet then, and he didn't need one. He preached one of the best sermons I ever heard right there in his front room.

"That old 'infidel,' as you seem to want to call him, is probably sitting up there in heaven, shaking his head over a preacher, some thirty-second-degree Masons, and a WMU president confabbing about whether he should have a church funeral or not. Now I didn't know Jake Spradling except for what I knew through Suzie, and from what I saw yesterday, and here's what I think happened, nearest I can figure it. When he stopped on that last ridge, sure as shootin' he knew his time had come. So he headed for the ravine to rendezvous with that lightning bolt alone, to save his wife and kids—and me and Ollie, too—from being burned along with him. Now, that's not too bad a man that would court certain death to save his family, is it? He may have been wrong about other things, but he was right at the very end.

"You're pestering yourselves about desecrating the church house with his body. Well, I agree with you, Jake doesn't deserve to have a church funeral. I'm not going to preach his funeral here, and I don't think I'll ask the folks down at Piney. We aren't going to sermonize on him inside *any* building. I say bury him right where he met God. He died clean before the Lord, just like old Uzzah, and if you want to, then stand around and wag over his grave there. For my part, it's hallowed ground."

Elmo said, "That's it, Preacher, I've had it up to here, and that is all I'm saying until Sunday." Him and Annie and Elmo all marched out to the pickup they'd come in, and Preacher followed them. Elmo jerked open the driver's door, and Annie got in the middle from the other side, then Wilbur. Well, they almost did. Somebody—most likely the McAnelly twins—had set a half-full can of beer on the seat and Annie slid it into Elmo and got them both wet. Elmo had been saving a choice word from his pre-conversion days, and decided to use it.

Preacher leaned his hands on the open driver's side window, sniffed, and said, "Well, Wilbur, is this one of those Baptist distinctives of yours? I will see you folks in church tomorrow, and I'll also see you at the funeral. I want you, Wilbur, and you, Elmo, to be two of the pallbearers. And I want you, Aunt Annie, to come and sit beside Suzie and help mind the kids. We'll start here at the church, then go to Jake's ravine for a graveside ceremony. I'm going to bed now. Good night."

I was never so proud of Preacher. It took a couple of weeks for Annie and Elmo and Wilbur to speak to him after this, but they were there at Jake's service.

19

RESTORATION

I reckon Blacksburg has had its share of hardheaded old coots, bootleggers, and grouches. Most of the time, though, you don't expect women to be that way, just the men. But then there was Miz Mary Scroggins, who lived right smack dab across the road from the church. God must have put her there to teach preachers humility.

One warm evening, Preacher was preaching right straight down the aisle, and Wes got up to open the door to get a breeze going, and there, across the road, up the Scroggins's place steps, she sat, swinging in that screechy swing. Straight as a rifle bore in a blue print dress, coal-black hair in spite of her forty-odd years, she stared right at Preacher and all he stood for—all the church stood for—looking in the very face of God and never blinking.

Preacher soon lost track of the gospel bullets he was firing, seeing as how they were flying across the street and ricocheting off her adamantine shield of a heart, to fall one by one in the dust. Pretty soon, he ran out of steam, wavered a bit, and started preaching to the left and then to the right. He took one more glance through the open door at his target, and came out from behind the pulpit to get out of the line of that silent return fire, but being young and seminary-trained, he couldn't breathe very long away from his desk. He had to retreat to the horns of the altar, where his notes were, and sure enough, as soon as he looked up, she was still sitting there in the squeaky swing, staring down his throat with a lazy insolence. I felt sorry for him, so I got up and shut the door.

Later, Preacher asked me about her, and I told him she hadn't been to church since early 1942. That was the year she and a former preacher of ours got mixed up in a bed quilt. The foo-fo-rah that followed split the town apart. Everybody thought it was Miz Mary who was at fault, since she had played pretty loose when she was in school, and of course, if our church had to have a scandal, they didn't want one started by their preacher. It came out later, when that preacher moved away and became a used car salesman, that there were several teenagers in Blacksburg who had been educated by the preacher, and not in Sunday School, neither. It was too late to backtrack, though, because the preacher had broke down and asked the church to forgive him, and so the church turned on Miz Mary and "churched" her. I really don't think it bothered her that the church withdrew fellowship from her so much, but that they would whitewash the preacher, who was every bit as guilty as she was.

She was so contemptuous of us and the church, she wouldn't even walk on the church side of the road. I once saw her walk through mud puddles on the far side of the road coming from the post office at Dolph's, when the ground was near dry on the church side. I think she was just being ornery when she took up with Hubert, just to see how she could vex Preacher.

Hubert Gann was a deacon who lived down in the Bend with Cory, his invalid wife. I use the word "invalid" advisedly, meaning what you'd think, of course, but she had about as healthy an unhealthy tongue as we've ever heard around these parts, and we aren't so backwards in those respects. It warn't even safe to leave black powder in reach of her voice. I remember old Hubert quoting that verse in deacons' meeting once about God not tempting us with more than a man could bear, but would provide a way to escape. He just took a strange way to escape it, and not one God would have had in mind, neither. He escaped right from the frying pan into the fire—right into the lap of a black widow spider.

I never saw a man so addled. He just up and parked on the Scroggins swing late one Saturday evening. Kept his hat on then, and most other times, too, but the darn fool was blind. He thought if he kept his hat on, everybody would think he was there on business. But everybody in town knew what was going on. Pretty soon the boys at the Lodge got nervous enough to talk about it, so then it was only a question of time before the church had to do something. By then, Hubert was sitting at the back of the church during services, coming in late and leaving early—except on Sunday night, when he would be the last one to leave. He would stack songbooks, close windows, and dawdle until everyone was gone. Then he would put on his hat, cross the road, and sit in the screechy swing while darkness fell.

Well, our church held a revival, and that red-haired Associational missionary from the neighboring Association came burning into Blacksburg, ready to Apostle Paul himself into our little Corinthian city. He didn't have to waggle his finger at the distant mountain and its lofty temple to Aphrodite neither—the mountain had come to him and was parked right across the street. Now some preachers are like old Spot, who is always feisty when there's a stray cat or dog in the yard; that is, until you open the door and say, "Sic 'em!" Then he suddenly starts working on a flea behind his ear. But I'll give Brother Bill his due—when he barked, he was ready to bite. He seen right away without being told, and there were plenty to tell him, that there were no young kids in the community ready for scaring into the Kingdom, so he lifted his sights to look for the hardened sinners of our town. And right straight down the aisle and across the road was a prime target.

If it hadn't been for what happened after, folks would still be saying what a great revival preacher he was. If you didn't already know, a great revival preacher is one who bloodies everybody's toes but yours. Well, everybody was happy that week, excepting for sore optic nerves from turning their eyes around without turning their heads, all to see Brother Bill's hot gospel projectiles aimed at that screechy porch swing over there in the dark and at Brother Hubert on the back row. It's to be said of the rascality and resiliency of the human spirit that old Hubert, he took it all pretty well, putting in his "Amen" almost as often as Wes and me and Elmo.

Well, Brother Bill zeroed in on Miz Scroggins. He tried pulling the trigger the last day before the closing service that night. We heard that exchange from where we were sitting at Dolph's store, except for when the train came through and drowned out the encores. Millard was so anxious to know what was being said and done that I thought he'd try to run between the rail cars to get over to where he could see and hear. But Preacher filled in the holes later, but even then he told it sober and pale, like a man who's just seen a hanging, or just realized he's stepped over a water moccasin without getting bit.

Seems he and Brother Bill were making the rounds of all the hard nuts in town, those who had sinned away their day of grace and those who had committed the unpardonable sin (though they couldn't have told you what it was), and the like. And there they were, cruising up to the front gate, scattering the chickens, and on up to the porch steps of Miz Scroggins's house. There warn't no answer at the front door, and Brother Bill was determined to face this particularly challenging sinner, so he and Preacher started around to the back to see if she was hanging out clothes or something. They didn't get much farther.

About the time they got up even with the back porch, she emptied a slop bucket (Wes always corrected me to say "jar," which I didn't appreciate, because he always trailed off into a giggle). Fortunately for Preacher, he was a little to the right and to the rear of Brother Bill when it happened. That missionary stopped dead, taking in the full significance of what had just happened, raised a finger to shake at her, and kind of froze in that posture. Miz Scroggins looked surprised for a minute—Preacher was sure it had been an accident—but then she let loose with a laugh as bitter as if it had come out of a quinine jar. She looked at Brother Bill, then at Preacher, and said, "Sorry, Brother Marshall, but I'm fresh out of perfume from my alabaster urn."

That's when the freight train came through. It was a short train, or else it saw what was going on in Blacksburg, and hurried on through. We sat up and paid full attention, for even though we've had a few tornadoes around here, we've never had the opportunity to observe one at leisure. Miz Scroggins reviewed Brother Bill's ancestry, weighed it in the balance and found it wanting. Brother Bill did a number of "Woe unto you, Jezebel!"s. She then scorned his manhood till even from where we were sitting in front of the store, we could see his neck light up brighter than his hair. He wiped his Bible off and began a Daily Bible Reading for her, which had to do with wanton women, but we couldn't hear very well for the mail train.

Well, by the time the mail train had gone, there warn't anyone in sight. Preacher said that before they huffed out of the yard, Brother Bill dared her to sit on the front porch that night—he was going to open up the church doors, pull out all the stops, and save her soul.

This was in the days before we had "Pack-a-Pew" night and Sunday School night and Hot Dog Supper night, but we didn't need any incentives that night—everybody was in church. Wes and I had taken up the Love Offering, and set it on the communion table, and were walking back to our seats by the door when I noticed something different across the way. Miz Scroggins was in her swing, all right—we could hear it. But tonight she also had the coal-oil lamps going in the dog-trot behind the swing, and I could see her real plain.

As I had a habit of doing, I sort of walleyed a glance over at Wes, and he skewered one back at me. We sat down, puzzled, bothered like mules in the pasture when there's ozone in the air. Sister Sara finished singing, and Brother Bill bounced up with his hackles up and a cleaned-up and perfumed Bible at the ready. I don't think I've ever seen a preacher come out of the starting blocks faster, except one a few years earlier who apparently had never studied the effects of energy upon mass, and hit the pulpit and kept right on going until he and the pulpit hit the floor in front of the rostrum. That made Aunt Annie so mad, seeing the pulpit that George W. Truett had preached from almost broken up on the floor, that she had us put C-clamps on the base from that day forward.

But as I was saying, he raised that Bible in one hand sort of low, and that Nathanic finger on the other hand sort of high, and announced vigorously, "My text tonight . . ." But then he hesitated. He kept his Bible under control, but that floating finger kind of fluttered down like a piece of down from a shot quail. ". . . is taken from—from—from the epistle of John."

Now that didn't sound exactly right to me and Wes and the others who had heard Brother Bill practicing early that afternoon—he'd worked up a good lather on a text out of Genesis about Sodom and Gomorrah—but we gave him a weak "Amen" anyway.

I knew that look on Brother Bill's face presaged an illumination of some kind of glory, but sure not the *shekinah* kind—in fact, he looked sort of scared. He continued, "The Lord has directed me to preach on Casting the First Stone." Well, I'd heard that song before, having sung it myself once or twice, so I just slewed myself around to see what Brother Bill saw across the way.

Sitting in that screechy swing, silhouetted against the dog-trot light, was Miz Scroggins, sure enough. She patiently held a twelve-gauge shotgun across her lap, ready to blow Brother Bill out through the baptistry at the first hint of rebuke.

After that I noticed that Preacher kept a watchful eye on the door, especially when it was open on a summer night. He saved his brimstone sermons for Sunday morning, which was when the sun was bearing down on Miz Scroggins's front porch, and she was sitting somewheres else.

20

TECHNOLOGY

Modern technology finally arrived in old Blacksburg, kicking and screaming. We were sitting out front of the store one Monday morning, waiting for the mail train, when Wes said, "There goes Preacher, roaring off down to the Bend with his wire recorder again. Have you ever tried to lift that contraption?"

Slim answered, "I shore did. It's like trying to pick up a dead sow, or load Aunt Rose in the ambulance back when she had her stroke—or is that being redundant?"

Preacher always wanted to be on the cutting edge of technology, but if it hadn't been for us old codgers, he would've been in the poorhouse. We didn't pay him much, but if we had, he would've just gone and squandered it on some newfangled toy. Like that slide projector he got to show pictures of the denuded Holy Land. It was always getting stuck, and Preacher would have to fish out a jammed slide with a hairpin. One night when he was trying to get from the pulpit to the projector, he got tangled up in the extension cord, and by the time Loren and Zane McAnelly had untangled him, the slide got overheated and burst into flame. Dolph was sitting on one side of the projector and jumped up in surprise, turning over the table and singe-ing Aunt Annie's hair. The last view we saw of the denuded Holy Land was a city at sunset. Wes, who had been dozing, woke up, leaned over and asked me, "Was that a picture of Sodom and Gomorrah when the fire fell?"

All this interest in technology started when Preacher went to Little Rock to the Baptist Bookstore for what was supposed to be a trip to pick up study course books for BYPU. He came home lugging this lead-lined wire recorder, with reinforced handles so two men could lift it. I don't know what they told him at the bookstore, but I looked on the bottom of the case to see if Thomas Alva Edison had autographed it.

Preacher's bright idea was that he could record the service, and take it to the shut-ins during the week, so they could listen to the brothers and sisters in Blacksburg holding forth on Sunday. Our homebound list included Aunt Rose, then Miss Betty Lou, then old man Tankersley down at road's end, with said road getting progres-sively worse at each stop.

Needless to say, Preacher's vision of what was going to be accom-plished was not exactly how it turned out. That wire recorder may have been intended for the bush country of Africa, but it couldn't negotiate those roads in the Bend. Preacher had to take it back to Little Rock every other week for repair. So, what was intended for the "evangelization of the heathen" became a roadblock in the schedules of many a potential convert, or parasitic believer. Whenever he took off to Little Rock to get his toy fixed, folks would complain, "Preacher ought to be here to carry me to the doctor to get my eyeball tested," or, "He's away from the church field too much. What if somebody needs him in an emergency?" or, "He's spending too much on gaso-line, roaring up and down Highway 64."

And the results of the Monday reenactments weren't very encouraging. Preacher strained his back lifting that machine out of the back of his Plymouth, where he carried it on a feather comforter to lessen the road shock, so I went with him to carry it in and out of the various homes. I thought to myself, usually while lugging that machine, "Saint Paul, you had it easy."

I could tell Preacher got a little water in his carburetor one morning, at the point where he was playing back a prided illustration of God's pursuing love, and Aunt Rose said, "That sounds like the Clendenning baby in the background. Ain't he just the cutest thing?" When we stopped at Miss Betty Lou's and had finished the rerun, she said, "Preacher, I need to ask you a question." Preacher thought he had a convert right there, and was already busy figuring out how to baptize a paraplegic, and said expectantly, "Yes, Miss Betty Lou?"

"Preacher, could you let me talk on that thing, too? I'd like to hear how I sound."

We batted a thousand that morning, when we ended up at old man Tankersley's, where he interrupted in the middle, asking, "Is that there machine made in Germany?"

Preacher missed the import of that question—old man Tankersley had lost two boys in World War Two, both on the German front—but he found out soon after.

One day not long after that, he had made his regular trip to Little Rock for wire recorder repairs, and stopped to see how far down on the list he was at the Volkswagen car agency. And lo and behold, a blue two-door VW had been turned back in by somebody who got tired of being honked at on the highway. They offered it to Preacher, and since a Volkswagen qualified as a technological advancement, Preacher spoke for it then and there.

He came home and asked me if I would go with him to Little Rock to pick up the wire recorder, and also go with him to look at a car. I didn't know that he had already bought it and had set up the loan at Worthen's in Little Rock. I was going to be his first guest rider—and the first Blacksburg native to ride in a Hitler car.

I know why he took me with him that day—not only had I loaded the wire recorder into the Plymouth for the trip to Little Rock, he probably figured what a chore it would be to load that contraption into the back seat of a two-door Hitler car. Whether he gave any thought to how he was going to load Aunt Rose into that miniature car for transportation back and forth to the clinic, I don't know. Of course, since Preacher never went anywhere by himself in a car with a woman other than his wife, that would mean that Sister Sara would get to ride in that tiny back seat.

I didn't put the recorder in the back seat. I put it in the front passenger seat, then went around and climbed into the back, behind Preacher, with my knees sort of tucked up under my armpits. I thought several times about asking Preacher if mental illness ran in his family, and did he realize what bringing a German car into Blacksburg would mean, but he was waxing eloquent about the high technology, and occasionally would demonstrate it by running the right wheels off the pavement, saying, "See how good it steers, even with half of it in the gravel?"

I just prayed. And when we got back to town, I thought about asking Preacher to let me off before we got to town, and let me walk, but I knew he had to unload that contraption, so I just hunkered down as we drove past the post office. I knew who would be sitting on the front porch of the store; I just hoped they couldn't see me.

Well, the next day was Sunday. I went to church early, did without my cigarette under the tree with the boys, and instead stood inside where I could peek through the window and watch.

Slim and Dolph were first. I could see them stalking around Preacher's new car like a hometown dog does when a new mutt moves in—all stiff-legged, and ready to start a war.

I eased the window up and heard Slim say, "Dolph, this looks like that car that drove by the store last night. Wes said it looked like Preacher driving, but I said it couldn't be—he ain't crazy, just over-educated."

Dolph let out a few choice words and said, "It's a German car, all right—a Hitler car. Who would be visiting Preacher from Germany?"

Well, the first big crisis with the car came at the Conoco station. We had two places to get gas in Blacksburg, but Preacher got his gas at the Conoco, because Oran Riggs, who owned the station, was on his prospect list. That day I was helping run the cash register while Oran was cooking those Seven for a Dollar hamburger specials, while his wife was abed sick. I saw Preacher pull up to the pump, set the brake, and get out. He walked around the car a couple of times, then cleaned the windshield a couple of times, waiting for someone to pump him some gas. I rang up a hamburger customer and went out to help him. We both walked around the car a couple more times. Finally, I said, "Preacher, if you'll just find the gas cap, I'll fill it for you. It does burn gas, don't it?"

Preacher turned sort of a technological red, and said, "Ollie, I can't find it!" So I went back in and got Oran, who came out, sort of disgusted. He took a look at the Hitler car and said, "Why don't you read the doggone manual? You're always reading one to me." We found the manual, and wouldn't you know, it was written in German. I asked Preacher if they taught German at the seminary, but by then, he was about to forget his religion altogether. Luckily, we found a picture that showed the gas cap under the turtle lid.

It was getting on toward the shank of the evening, so I tried to hurry. I let Preacher insert the nozzle, which was a mistake. He ran it over, and there was all this gas sloshing around in the turtle, soaking into all the cracks. I made a mistake, too, so we each had one: I didn't see the hold-open rod in the failing light, and crimped the turtle lid good and proper. It didn't show too much, and besides, it let some of those gasoline fumes out at the crack. Even so, he drove around addled on fumes for weeks after that. I allowed to Preacher that if German automotive technology was so all-fired great, how come they didn't put the gas cap on the outside where it should have been. Preacher just rolled his eyes and said, "You don't understand aerodynamics." I grumbled back under my breath, "You don't understand displacement, but you're going to learn as soon as you try to take Aunt Rose to the doctor."

The next crisis came when he took his recorded Sunday service down to old man Tankersley in his Hitler car, only to get run off the premises with a twelve-gauge. That was when he found out about the Tankersley boys who died in the war. Preacher wrote out a drop slip on the shut-in list for him.

Over the next few weeks, that car got introduced to the Bend in a big way. One night somebody let the air out of the tires during prayer meeting. Nobody would park next to the thing, to avoid guilt by association. Another night, during a Pie Supper at the school, where Preacher was supposed to give the invocation, some objectors (I assume at least four) picked that car up and wedged it between two trees, bumper to bark. Preacher had to walk home that night, but at least he was full of pie. Next day he got me to help him crosscut-saw one of those trees down so he could drive away. He wanted that tree down in a hurry, before many folks saw it. But shoot, it didn't matter; everybody already knew about it, and most had seen it. Preacher got so worked up bucking that saw that he never noticed he was whipping his bare arms through poison ivy vines. He did notice later.

One Monday morning, Millard stepped out from sorting mail and said, "Preacher, why don't you just leave the recorder in the front seat of your car, and stop hand-carrying it around? You can just get a couple of us to carry the car into the church each Sunday and set it by the pulpit where you can record."

I guess Preacher finally got fed up with it, or maybe Sister Sara got tired of having to fold herself into the back every time she got in, since the wire recorder had to stay in the front passenger seat. Great was the relief all over Blacksburg the day he came back from recorder repairs in Little Rock with a four-door Dodge station wagon, a couple of years older than the Plymouth he'd traded for the Volkswagen, but in real nice condition.

Sometimes technology ain't worth the trouble.

21

PIE SUPPER

By the second year after Preacher hove onto the scene, he had covered a lot of ground visiting folks, but somehow he hadn't made it out to the Beulah place. It was inevitable that sooner or later he would, and sure enough, he got them excited about starting back to church.

Well, I'd heard that song before, but didn't want to bust Preacher's bubble, so I let him learn the tune by himself. You would have had to see the Beulah place to believe it. Old Heck Beulah built his house out of salvaged ammunition boxes that he hauled in by the truckload from the Jacksonville ammunition plant. It made a pretty interesting house.

Preacher was waxing enthusiastic about that house. He said, "You know, that Heck Beulah is the very image of ingenuity and efficiency." That made old Heck and Miz Samantha proud as peacocks. Then, one Sunday, when Sister Sara was out of town at a Woman's Missionary Union doings, they up and invited Preacher and me for Sunday dinner. I knew what was coming, but there was no way I was going to miss Preacher's inauguration.

Sunday came, and there we were, sitting in Heck's living room, and Preacher was walking around looking at the walls, with Heck explaining again about them ammo boxes. Preacher was oohing and aahing about the handy shelves on every wall to set things, and me, I just kept a wary eye on the kitchen. They say the mills of God grind slow, but mighty sure. I'd say the same for Miz Samantha Beulah's cooking—it may not come fast, but there ain't no escaping it.

We sat down at the kitchen table, and Preacher said the blessing. At the "Amen," Preacher looked up and there was Miz Samantha's pet rooster perched smack dab on the table, looking over this new member of the persecuting class; he'd done seen several of his feathered cohorts enter the ministry, and he just didn't understand the call. Preacher had thanked God for the chicken, but he didn't expect to see a live one sitting with the salt and pepper shakers. He shooed, and that old rooster promptly flew over the stove and landed on the wood box. I think they call it the domino theory, but we called it the wood-pile theory after that. When that rooster settled, the stovewood started settling, too, and Miz Samantha's pet pig came squealing out from under the stove, went under Preacher's chair and knocked one leg loose as he headed for the open door. That brightened up the meal considerably.

So, Heck and Samantha sat there and grinned at Preacher, whose reputation as a hearty eater had preceded him (it sort of runs in the breed, I reckon). He loaded up his plate and went to work enthusiastically, but his enthusiasm took a header on the first mouthful. As I have previously stated, I can be a man of few words, and on this subject, I just said 'em. Miz Samantha made sure that any diminution of the various kinds of food on his plate was replaced according to the doctrine of "pressed down, shaken, and running over." I had allowed as how my ulcer was acting up, so they had set me with sweet milk and crackers, and I was enjoying things considerable.

Anyhow, there we sat—Mr. and Mrs. Beulah, Preacher, and me, just pulling up to the top of the grade, Preacher thought, and ready for the downhill slide. Miz Samantha hopped up to go get the cake, while Preacher got a firm hold on one horn of his dilemma. He was known all over the Bend as a *par excellence* cake lover (though he did a pretty good job on all kinds of sweets), and he knew he had his work cut out for him if the cake was anything like the meal.

He tried to let go of that horn and hop to the other, which was the deep-seated evangelical belief that there was no such thing as "bad" cake. And I have to give Miz Samantha credit; it was a fine-looking cake, piled with chocolate icing, and so fresh the flies hadn't even walked on it yet.

She served Preacher a mountainous slab and then set back to watch. This was virgin country to me from here on in. I'd never seen one of her cakes before, and this cake was kind of coarse-looking inside, with big bubble holes in it, but it was nice and yellow like corn meal— which, in fact, it turned out to be, and that without sugar. My slewing eye had seen her mixing up the icing—Tucker shortening and cocoa, with no sugar—while Preacher was explaining Open Communion to Mr. Beulah. Preacher did his best. I had noticed at other times that he always saved the parts with the icing till last, sort of like the dessert of the dessert to him. He had saved this chocolate icing for last, too, and I could see he thought his redemption was drawing nigh. He rolled the first bite around in his mouth an uncommon long time, and conversation got kind of still. I had to pick up the ball while Preacher finished up in Gethsemane.

Miz Beulah said proudly, "You know, that's the first cake I ever made. I knowed you like cake, Preacher, so I fixed it special for you."

I said, "Is that right? I declare, I never would have known it. Did you hear that, Preacher? She said this is the first cake she ever made. Don't that beat all?"

Preacher's eyes had a glaze on them as he rolled them in my direction, completely missing Miz Beulah's move to cut him another wedge, until it was too late. Before he could raise his fork in self defense, she had plopped it on his plate. About that time, I had to get up and help the pig back up the stump step into the kitchen, and then I said I thought I'd mosey on down to the barn to look at the corn crib they were building out of ammunition boxes. My eyes seemed to be bothering me about then, and I needed to sneeze.

It took Preacher awhile to forgive me.

Anyway, time came for our annual Pie Supper. This was what some people would call a Box Supper, 'cause sure enough, there were boxes, and the young men would bid to get their girl's box of chicken and trimmings. But we didn't stop there. Getting your best girl's box supper is nice, but getting her pie as well is a pure-D delight, so we did it right at Blacksburg. We even got the auctioneer from up at the peach shed to come and auction off our wares. Everybody came rolling in, bringing large boxes which contained chicken and the like, and flatter, fancier boxes containing the cakes and pies.

Preacher, that efficient eating machine, was anticipating an evening of ecstasy, as every family would invite him to share a bit of the prize pie or cake they'd snagged. He had gone across the road to open the parsonage for use of the indoor bathroom, and when he got back he stopped at the front door and looked expectantly over the crowd to the rows of boxes up behind the pulpit. Then I saw him sort of freeze, and a sick smile spread over his face. Navigating toward him was a beaming Miz Samantha Beulah, with Heck bringing up the rear with a big grin. "Betcha can't guess which box is mine, Preacher," she said. "I may just tell you which one it is, so's you can eat with us."

Now that two-horned bull was first cousin to the dilemma Preacher had faced awhile back. Preacher blinked like he didn't ever want to know which box they had brought. He must have had a little Presbyterian blood in him, and he just knew he was predestined to bid and win the very box he didn't want. Of course, the Free Will Baptist in him was lusting to know which box it was, so he could, under any circumstances, steer clear of it.

Miz Beulah was just about to capture him with the awful knowledge, when the auctioneer started. Now I warn't real sure myself which box had the lethal load in it, so I just shrugged my shoulders at Preacher when he gave me this little desperate poke in the ribs. I said, "Preacher, what you need is a Urim and Thummin."

Preacher lucked out on the first offering—he got Aunt Annie's dinner box, and would have considered it God's grace, seeing as she was about the best cook in the church. But he didn't enjoy it at all. I think he knew that the only way to balance out the providence of God in "sending the rain on the just and the unjust" was for him to receive the good cooking of Aunt Annie, and pay the price for the just desserts.

Well, he tried. He bid so high on some of them boxes, if he hadn't been the Preacher and already married, someone would've known for sure he was trying to beat their time. But it didn't work—he couldn't buy a pie for any money. Finally, we were all looking at the last box on the bench. I looked over at Miz Samantha and thought, "Well, Preacher, you're right: It is only through much tribulation that we may enter the Kingdom." It was hers, all right. Preacher knew that when he bid two bits, and got so flustered at no competition, that he raised his own bid.

At last it was time to untie all those bows, bless the food, and dig in. Preacher, of course, did the praying, and he prayed, all right—all the way around the walls of Jericho, to Greenland's icy mountains, and was about to inventory God's storehouse, when he said, "Hallelujah!" and opened his eyes with a big smile.

"Folks," he said, "before we eat, let's raffle off a pie for Foreign

Missions. Now you know how much I like pie, but I'm willing to make a sacrifice—I'm going to put my unseen prize on the block. I always wanted to be an auctioneer, but couldn't talk fast enough. Lon, would you let me auction off this box?"

And I thought, "Well, Preacher, you may not talk fast, but in a press you think pretty fast." Of course, I knew exactly what he was doing—just double-insuring himself against having to personally untie the lid to that culinary Pandora's box. He did a tolerable job of auctioneering, and the people responded. We got a nice offering for Miz Lottie Moon, the missionary lady in China. Human beings can do things they have never done before when things get desperate.

I told Preacher later, while he was making the circuit, sampling pie from variouses and sundries, "Preacher, you sure got the missionary spirit. You made that there Miz Beulah so happy being a part of taking the gospel to the heathen, she's beside herself. She's invited you and me back for dinner again this coming Sunday."

"I'm sorry, Ollie, I can't do it," he answered, and I gave him a big grin, knowing-like. But he seemed real serious, and he kind of wall-eyed me over to a spot out of the middle of the fellowshipping. There, he said in a low voice, "We got a call from the Foreign Mission Board last night, and their field representative will be stopping by Sunday on his way to Nashville. You know our hearts have always been on the mission field, and we can't miss this opportunity to see if they have a place of service for us."

Suddenly, I warn't hungry anymore, and ducked out to the front yard to roll a smoke.

22

THE LODGE AND THE CRAFT

It seemed like Preacher got his metal annealed after Jake's funeral. He didn't jump through hoops for Aunt Annie no more, and he spent less time coddling the old guard. I'd like to think it was his time in the Lodge that done it, but it was probably just his curled lip maturing.

Speaking of the Lodge, his petition to join came about in an interesting way. At the time it happened, Preacher was wading his way through the Old Testament with a series of sermons and spent one particular Sunday dealing with Solomon's Temple. You never saw people so intent on what he was saying. Even Preacher noticed the people leaning forward to listen, and he stopped several times to study his notes, trying to figure out what he was saying that was so interesting.

I felt my hackles rising at what he was revealing, and I could see several of the brethren in the Lodge getting angry, particularly Slim, who swelled up like a toad. Wes leaned over to me and said, "He ain't got no right telling about that!" I looked over at Aunt Annie and her cadre of WMUers. They were leaning forward, drinking in every word, nodding their heads like chickens at a waterhole.

After the service, Preacher was standing at the door shaking everybody's hand as they shuffled out, as was his custom. I was hanging back so I could hear and see what was going on. Slim, who was Worshipful Master, Millard, who was Senior Warden, and Elmo, who was Chaplain, all stalked out like ramrods. Elmo and Wilbur homed in on Preacher together, and Elmo demanded, "Who gave you that book on the Scottish Rite?"

Preacher looked kind of dazed, but the line moved on, and some of the women started saying things like, "Preacher, I always wondered what the Lodge was about, and you done explained it pure and simple," and "I shore do appreciate you telling us what they do in those upstairs Lodge meetings." I could see Preacher was flabbergasted. He said to me as we shut the windows, "Ollie, what on earth happened today?"

I said, "Preacher, if you are going to meddle with the secrets of Freemasonry, you are going to lose a lot of friends around here." Preacher looked at me with eyes as big as Wes's and said, "Ollie, I don't know what you're talking about. I just dealt with the scriptures that describe Solomon's Temple and its craftsmanship. What's wrong with that?"

"Well, Preacher, I'm going to invite myself over for Sunday dinner, and as soon as we're through, we'll talk about it."

So I went over to the parsonage, and after the meal, Sister Sara took the leftovers and the dirty dishes out into the kitchen, and Preacher laid his Bible out on the table. When he started showing me his notes and references, I was amazed—I didn't know all that stuff was in the Bible. My aggravation dissolved and I began to laugh. "Preacher, we men folks, to a man, thought you had got hold of one of those illegal books revealing all of the Masonic secrets. All you done was read the Bible, and you know as much about Freemasonry as a thirty-second-degree Mason. No wonder you got everybody all stirred up this morning. I can't wait to get to the post office in the morning and tell the boys what I've learned today. Who knows, they may decide to let you and Sister Sara stay in Blacksburg another week or two."

A cloud came over Preacher's face as he said, "Well, Ollie, you know we're not going to be here forever, anyway. If we can just get through all the paperwork and interviews, we hope to get an appointment at the next meeting of the Foreign Mission Board."

I warn't so happy at that reminder, but I made a secret resolve to get Preacher dressed out in a Masonic apron before he left. This turned out to be a real challenge, because every time the Lodge came up in a conversation, Preacher would quickly change the subject. I never pestered him about it, because that's not the way of the Lodge. But one day down at Dolph's, Slim said something about the Eastern Star ladies having a supper honoring the Masons, and Preacher got up and took his soda pop out on the porch of the store. I followed him, and finally asked him straight out, "Preacher, what *is* it about Freemasonry that gets you so riled up?"

Preacher leaned on the rail and took a swig of his soda pop, and asked, "Ollie, how many men in our church are Masons?"

"I guess just about everybody, except maybe old man Stonaker," I answered.

"Well, that figures. Let me tell you something about my family. My dad, all during my growing up, never mentioned his own dad and his involvement in the Lodge. I wondered why, until one time when I was about twelve, I was sitting on the front porch after dark, playing with my dog, and I heard two of my aunts, who were visiting us, talking in the front room. It seems my grandfather had up and run off with an opera lady, leaving Grandma with a passel of kids to raise. My dad had to quit school, and started work in a confectionary to help make ends meet.

"Then, one winter day, two men rode up in the yard, called my Grandma and the kids out, and without getting off their horses or even tipping their hats, one of them read some kind of legal eviction notice. They were Grandpa's buddies from the Lodge. They beat it out of there when my dad, who wasn't more than twelve or thirteen, came out of the house with the shotgun, but the next Saturday, they came in wagons and loaded up Grandma's belongings and her brood, and hauled them out of town to a sharecropper's cabin. The home place was sold at auction to pay the taxes, and what was left over, the county judge, who was the Worshipful Master of the Lodge, sent to Grandpa and his opera lady. Grandma died before that winter was out, and the kids were scattered to the winds.

"Well, as I was listening to my aunts rehashing the past, my dog snapped at me. I realized that I had his collar twisted up in my hands, and was slowly choking him. I buried my head in my dog's forgiveness, and after awhile fell asleep. I never asked my dad about his growing up after that, and he carried the hatred and contempt of the Lodge all his life. I guess it just sort of rubbed off on me, too."

"Preacher," I said, "that's a sorry story if ever I heard one, and it makes me kinda sick to hear it. But you're in danger of throwing the baby out with the bath water. Those buddies of your Grandpa's were just rascals who happened to be Masons. There's lots of fine men in the Lodge; that's really the whole point of it. Don't dump the whole barrel just because one bad apple showed up in it. Think about joining the Lodge. I'll bet you'll find a lot of men will listen to you that never would otherwise. Didn't you say in your sermon the other night that Paul became all things to all men just so he would be listened to? Why, I've heard that Lodge members in a strange country can just give a distress signal, and up will step a Mason to give him aid."

Preacher looked thoughtful, polished off his Nehi, and rubbed his chin. "Well, Ollie, you know, that might not be bad insurance for a missionary preacher to have in whatever heathen country he ends up in. Besides, it would sure make Sara's dad, who's in the Lodge in Texarkana, happier to have me as a son-in-law. What do I have to do to become a Mason?"

Well, it took some doing, what with first one of us, then another, driving him down a country lane at dusk or after dark, then parking and going over the material that he had to learn by heart. We had to keep the windows up, so the skeeters wouldn't completely eat us up, but at least between Slim, Wes, Millard, Dolph, and myself, we only gave blood every fifth day—Preacher had to fight off those dive bombers every night. I think they were the reason he learned the rites in record time—or maybe he crammed to get it over with, so he'd be ready when the Mission Board gave him and Sister Sara the green light.

Naturally, his initiation didn't go altogether by the script.

The date was set for Preacher's induction. I noticed that the women folks were pretty much in a dither at the time, incessantly curious about what was taking place in the room over Dolph's store, and hopeful that Preacher would let slip some more of the Masonic "secrets" during the course of his preparation for the degrees.

Even Aunt Annie was frustrated. She kept after Wes like a sore tooth, probing for information, listening up in the middle of the night, hoping he would talk in his sleep, but to no avail. Wes had played second fiddle in that relationship since the day he met Annie, but in things pertaining to the Lodge he knew he held an ace card, and he warn't going to play it.

On the night of the induction, the old codgers in the Lodge were in fine fettle, and all of us were proud out of measure. I did have a fleeting thought that something was bound to be different about this initiation. It just had to be, if Preacher's penchant for crises held true.

The Lodge Room was located over the back of the store, and there was only one way to get to it—up a flight of stairs behind a door that was kept padlocked. When we went up there that night, we didn't yet know that someone—most likely our resident twin terrors, Zane and Loren, though we never did find out for sure—had sneaked into the building the night before through an upstairs window, and since they couldn't get into the store past the locked stairway door, had pulled up some of the floor boards in the closet in the Lodge Room and dropped into the feed room below. Dolph said later that he'd noticed several plugs of tobacco missing, a feed sack broken open, and the stick that kept the back window locked was ajar.

So, we were just as much in the dark as he was when we led a blindfolded Preacher to the closet, opened the door, pushed him in, and closed it. He was to wait there until the proper time. It never came.

We heard this noise from the closet, where we had instructed Preacher to be absolutely quiet. Wes said, "Ain't that just like a preacher—you can't trust them to stay quiet for a minute!"

The noise changed to a groan, then a muffled crash. We all looked at each other; there warn't nothing in our ceremony to handle this contingency. Elmo growled and asked, "There ain't no deep water in that closet, is there?" Wilbur lamented, "We done lost half our Baptist distinctives in the church because of him, and now he's working on our Lodge." Slim, the Worshipful Master, looked at me and said in a weary tone, "Ollie, go see what you can do to get this train back on the track."

I got one of the Coleman lanterns we were using for light from where it hung on the wall, opened the closet door, and peered in. "Preacher . . . ?" I asked. No answer.

Wilbur pushed me out of the way, saying, "Let me get that fool out of there." The next thing I saw was Wilbur dropping through the floor that was no longer there. He let out a startled yell, then a strangled scream, when he spraddle-legged the floor joist.

It took four of us to lift Wilbur off the joist and lay him on the floor, and he curled up into a fetal position. I figured we needed to leave him alone for awhile, knowing from experience that there is nothing you can do for a man in that condition to make him feel better.

So the rest of us thundered down the stairs, and we burst into the feed room with my lantern held high. There we found Preacher, sitting up on a broken bag of shorts with his head in his hands, but with the blindfold still on. Wes jumped in ahead of me to check on him and stepped smack dab on a square feed shovel laying on the floor. Yep, it sure did! That shovel handle flew up in the dusty darkness and whammed Wes right between the eyes, and down he went. I backed away, and told Slim, who was right behind me, "Don't move—it's Preacher, sure enough. Anything or anybody that gets close to him is taking a terrible risk. Besides, I think he's going to be all right."

Our candidate swayed a little from side to side, and asked weakly, "Is this a standard part of the initiation?"

By the time we got Wes revived and helped him and Preacher back up the stairs, Wilbur had crawled over to his appointed corner. We didn't have any visitors that night, so I suppose the variations of the ceremony we suffered through never went on our record. Preacher probably thought it was our usual modus operandi, although I think he got an inkling that it was out of the ordinary the following Monday at mail call.

That was when Wilbur was able to walk, in a strange, splay-legged sort of way, and was in the store when Preacher arrived. Nobody but Masons were in the store at the time, so when Wilbur got up and assayed to go over to the cracker barrel, Preacher noticed his progress and asked, "Wilbur, is that one of those Masonic distress signals?"

23

BATH TIME

Sometimes you think you know pretty nearly everything there is to know about somebody, and it isn't until you're about to wave them goodbye that you find out you don't. What I found out, and Preacher 'fessed up to one day when we were making one last run at hunting arrowheads, was that Blacksburg was his second choice of church job when he got out of the seminary. We were sitting in the shade, easing our back muscles, when he told me how he found out that his second choice was God's first choice.

Preacher said he was up to preach in view of a call at this little church out from Mount Ida, on the Caddo River, right before he married Sister Sara. He poured everything he had into one Sunday morning sermon. That was safe to do, because he couldn't preach that night—they didn't have electric lights down there. So he used up all those Texas illustrations about cows and round-ups, and told a couple of stories about trains, trestles, and clotheslines, and finished it off with the old violin and a bridge builder. The church decided to call him, since he sure did know his gospel.

Well, there warn't any place for him to stay, so Mr. and Miz

Robbins, who were mainstays in the church, said they would put him up. He was going to stay a week, look over the field, and preach the next Sunday. He said Miz Robbins was skinny as a rail, spry as a mule, and could out-talk, out-walk, out-work, and out-pray anyone he ever saw. She'd get up at dark before the mist began to rise on the river, put three meats, biscuits, cornbread, two pies, and assorted vegetables on the table along with what you and I would call sufficient ordinary vittles, then she'd milk, and clean her house—that last not amounting to much except bed-making, sweeping chicken mess off the porch, and washing dishes. All of this she'd get done while Mr. Robbins was groping around, trying to hook a claw into his 'nalls strap. About the time he'd get this full meal down with a pot of coffee, she'd throw a tablecloth over the whole caboodle, and they were off for the fields, hoes and Tucker buckets in hand, and it wouldn't even be rosy dawn yet.

Well, this was what Preacher moved into, which was a far cry from his hoot-owl habits. Miz Robbins ensconced him across the dog-trot in this single bedroom with a nice introduction: "This here's your bed, Preacher. It's a tad bit high, but you'll sink in that feather bed. This is where Pap killed hisself, right here in this bed. See here, he sat right here, put that shotgun that's hanging over the door there in his mouth, and toed the trigger. Blowed his brains all over the ceiling. I shore do miss him. Well, good night, Preacher, I'll get you up for breakfast. We get up a mite early around here."

Preacher said he didn't go to sleep too early that night, so when Miz Robbins tin-panned his door next morning, he disentangled himself from the rafters and blearied himself out into the dog-trot. Breakfast was half over, and Preacher kept looking around for the folks he supposed were going to eat that feast, but whoosh, the tablecloth got spread, and they left him for the fields. He followed them out onto the porch and asked, "Where can I shave and take a bath?"

Miz Robbins turned and looked at him like he was addled. "Bath? This ain't Saturday. Well, if you want to, the river's down that-a-way."

Preacher found the river before the gray light was gone, pulled off his shoes and hobbled into the cold water. He had to take a britches-legs bath that morning out of pure modesty. But after walking the hills, visiting the different homes, and pretty near wearing out his city shoes, he was getting near to needing a real bath. Come Saturday morning, he was so wore out with walking over those mountain rock trails, getting up in the wee hours to eat, and staring at a nightmare ceiling of scattered brains, that he overslept a bit, and the Robbinses had already departed for the field when he hit the floor. He wolfed down some breakfast and took off for the river, determined to have a good bath, ice water or not, because tomorrow was Sunday, and he was having no trouble sniffing his own trail.

A little gray light was left when he got to the riverbank. He deposited his clothes on a large rock, draped a towel around his neck, and egg-shelled over the rocky bottom, Lifebuoy in hand. He had not known the river was so shallow out so far, so he waded a distance farther, the visibility in the swirling mist such that his modesty was quite relaxed.

Then, in one of those vagaries of whimsical Mother Nature, the mist chose that particular moment to lift, and what was predawn darkness became clear morning light. This was no doubt startling, and probably with so much distance back to his clothes rock, he panicked a bit. Panic in a flowing, rock-bottomed stream is not conducive to balance, and his sudden ablution also was not conducive to quiet. In the thrill of the moment, he lost his towel in the current, and was simultaneously chilled at the trill of laughter from behind him, too near to be mistaken. He slowly turned around to see with unbelieving eyes that he was in a bend of the Caddo which passed right through the town of Mount Ida. Several early-morning-riser parishioners were pointing and tittering in his direction. Thoroughly horrified and confused at how a trip by road from town that consumed some six or seven miles had culminated in landing him right back in town like a descaled minnow in a fishbowl, he beat a hasty retreat. Like a pilgrim headed for the horns of the altar in a far-off City of Refuge, he skittered across the water, carefully wielding his Lifebuoy as a shield against the darts of the adversary.

Well, he told me that he just kept going. I remember hearing about that time that some trucker at the Conoco café talked about picking up an educated hitchhiker who hunkered down in the cab as they went through Mount Ida. They still talk out there about that preacher who, as far as they could tell, must have preached himself dry with one sermon, and tried to soak up another one from the river.

That was why he seemed so relieved to find out there was a real bathroom in the Blacksburg parsonage—and why he eventually lantern-jawed the church into digging a septic tank and putting one in the church house, too.

24

POUNDING

Finally, the day came when Preacher and Sara did what few preachers at Blacksburg Baptist Church have had the opportunity to do: They resigned without benefit of a proper firing. They asked the congregation to bless them as they answered the Lord's call to the foreign mission field. It was a surprise to everyone but me, but it still warn't easy to hear. They would be with us for two more Sundays, and then they would move to Atlanta for a year of training before they got their appointment.

Remember Brother Cullen, the missionary from the Amazon who just about got undone by the McAnelly twins? Well, he evidently recognized Preacher's missionary potential, and gave him one of his nicest recommendations. Or maybe he thought it would be fitting revenge for Preacher to spend some time simmering in a Pygmy stewpot. But Preacher and Sara wouldn't be going to the jungle—they would be "urban" missionaries in the city of Lima, Peru.

We had run off so many preachers before, or they ran off before we could get in gear, that we didn't know how to handle a peaceful departure. But finally, the WMUers got the ball rolling and we targeted the Marshalls's last Sunday night with us for a pounding. Never mind that poundings are supposed to happen when someone arrives, not when he departs. We had already given Preacher and Sara one of those when they first came, to stock up their pantry with "a pound of this, and a pound of that." I remember, because Preacher was so proud of the home-cured ham that Elmo gave him and Sister Sara.

One advantage of staying put where you were raised is knowing where to eat and where not to eat. Preacher invited several folks, me included, for Sunday dinner after that first pounding, but he couldn't find any takers—everybody sensed somehow that he would inaugurate that ham. Elmo was pretty well-known for passing off his old dried-up hams on preachers and evangelists. He got rid of them that way—the hams, that is—plus, he considered it a charitable contribution. I saw Wilbur walking down to the Conoco station to get a sack of those Seven for a Dollar burgers about mid-afternoon that Sunday, and he said he saw Preacher out on his screened-in back porch, sawing and hammering something. He muttered something to me about "working on the Sabbath," and "losing our Baptist distinctives," but I knew what had happened. Preacher and Sara were having a late lunch that day, after they finally got that home-cured ham of Elmo's sawed up.

The next morning, I saw Preacher at Dolph's store while we were waiting for the mail to be put up. He got up three times to get a drink out of the water bucket, and I allowed as how he was going to get foundered. Then Elmo came in to get a new slop jar for his mother, and having made his purchase, got ready to walk back home, which was about three miles. Preacher jumped up and said, "Come on, Brother Elmo, walk up to the parsonage with me, and I'll drive you home right after lunch."

I heard later that Elmo asked Preacher on the way to the parsonage what Sister Sara was fixing for lunch. Preacher said innocently, "Oh, probably just some sandwiches." Well, they had sandwiches all right—sawdust ham sandwiches out of Elmo's ham. Preacher told me that Sara didn't bother to put any salad spread on them like she usually did, which would have helped keep the ham between the bread slices and made it easier to swallow. He said Elmo drank all his sweet milk, and asked for two more glasses before they were through. Then, as he and Preacher rose to go to the car, Sister Sara sweetly handed him a substantial package, saying, "Brother Elmo, I fixed a couple of sandwiches for you and Miz Pearl to have for supper—I hope you enjoy them as much as we have."

Elmo didn't give Preacher any more hams.

Well, we were all kind of shocked at who showed up at Preacher and Sara's farewell pounding. Old man Stonaker didn't bring any food, but he gave Preacher a brown paper bag tied with string, and labeled "The Origin of the Species." Preacher opened it with a jaundiced eye, thinking, "Here we go again with evolution and Darwin." But inside was a brand-new King James Bible, Red Letter Edition. Old man Stonaker told a surprised Preacher, "I finally found out where I came from in there, but not only that, where I'm going."

The McAnelly twins brought a Bull Durham sack full of arrow points and tearfully gave them to Preacher. He put one arm around a twin each, and they went over in the corner and laid the relics out on a pew so he could admire them.

Even Rat and Ethyl came, in spite of being Church of Christers. Ethyl brought a cake, and somebody nudged Preacher and said he ought to cut it now, since Rat and Ethyl might get a little uncomfortable among so many Baptists and decide to leave. Preacher did the honors, and sliced off a big wedge before it got out of his sight. But his knife hit something inside the cake, and when he unearthed it, he found a vintage bed caster. He and Rat and Ethyl started them another case of the "sillies" over that, until Elmo harrumphed them quiet.

There was plenty of food, serious food, plus canned greens and sausage, most of it in fruit jars. Nobody brought any jelly, though, because the news was pretty common around these parts that Preacher and Sara wouldn't ever need any more jelly, particularly plum.

We were all having a good time, when things got quiet at the door. That wave of quietness quickly washed down the aisle and surrounded us down by the pulpit. We looked up to see what was going on at the door, and there stood a hesitant Miz Mary Scroggins, with a hat on her head, eyes drilled straight ahead to where Preacher stood. She was locked onto him like if she ever took her eyes off him, she would sink into the abyss. She was also carrying a box with a bow on it.

I could see the WMU troops maneuvering over at the side aisle for a flanking action. All the men folks melted away and left Preacher alone by the communion table where the pounding stuff was stacked. I could see real good because I was over by the open window, ready to dive out if I saw she was packing heat. But Miz Mary said, "Preacher, I want you to have this." Preacher took it, turned it over ginger-like, but two things were apparent: One was that she expected him to open it. The second was that Preacher didn't have the slightest inclination to open it. Well, I wouldn't have opened it, either.

But Preacher evidently stretched his faith to the limit, and said, "Mary, why don't you open it for me—I'm so clumsy." The last half of that was certainly the truth. She took out of the box a real pretty vase of dried and silk flowers. I guess she got flustered, 'cause the vase slipped. She juggled it, then she and Preacher both grabbed for it, but it was too late. They got their hands tangled up together, and the vase crashed at their feet. Mary burst into tears—I reckon no one knew she had any. Well, Preacher kept hold of her hand with one of his, and bent down to pick up the flower arrangement, minus the vase. "Mary, Mary, don't cry," he said gently. "These flowers are a treasure, a very special treasure. I'll keep them as long as I live and have them put on my grave. Sara, honey, let Mary sit over there with you."

A lot of people seemed to be having allergy problems about then, wiping their eyes or nose, or clearing their throat. Events like that probably don't seem important to outsiders, but to those of us who lived in Blacksburg, and knew all its little scandals and stories, that broken vase of artificial flowers still conjures up a lump in the throat, and filters down through the years as one of our lives' most precious memories.

Millard broke the awkward silence, saying, "Sister Sara, sing us one more song, for old times' sake." I guess he thought that would cheer everybody up, but people just started boo-hooing. But Sara had barely got finished with the first, second, and last verses when we heard a racket outside—a couple of backfires and some hollering—and in came a hay wagon full of Piney folks and Flat Rockers. On our side of the creek! Wes whispered, "Oh, shoot, I didn't lock my front door." Aunt Annie drew herself up with a sniff, and we could see her feathers rising up protectively. She allowed as how "This is *our* preacher, and they don't have any right barging into our affairs."

I guess we all saw that night what Preacher had done while among us. No, he didn't change how we felt—at least, not all of us, but he showed us we could act different if we would, and let our feelings get adjusted later. He embraced us all, Blacksburg, Piney, and Flat Rock; shaped notes or newfangled round ones; and whether we were saturated with Baptist distinctives or moonshine, he loved us.

After I helped Preacher carry all the fruit jars over to the parsonage later that night, and we had gone back to close the church windows, I said, "Preacher, I want you to promise me that you'll come back to Blacksburg to preach my funeral. If you're down there in Peru, I'll have them put me on ice until you get a furlough."

Preacher didn't say nothing; he just turned and put his arms around me and gave me a big old hug. I hadn't never hugged a grown man, except my own son, but in a way, this Gene Marshall kid of a preacher was like my own flesh and blood, and it seemed real natural to hug back.

"I'll give you that promise," he said when we let each other go, and his lip curled up as he added, "if you'll swap me your promise that there won't be any flowers around the pulpit."

"Preacher," I said, "you're learning. You're learning."

EPILOGUE

The years have come and gone, just like the trains that used to interrupt Preacher's Sunday night sermons. The lazy, temperamental River has been tamed by the Arkansas River Lock and Dam System, and its spawn of fishing john-boaters has been supplanted by speeding pleasure boats. We don't raise peaches commercially any more, but the chicken plant is now part of a vast corporate poultry empire. Almost everybody has an indoor bath, and there are even streetlights down our blacktopped main street. There's still a Conoco station at the edge of town, but now it's a truck stop and an Interstate highway roars by it.

Along with the years, others have followed. Wes is gone; Annie seemed to hang on forever, but now she's gone, though sometimes I can still hear her setting someone or another straight. Slim is in a rest home in Arizona, and Dolph and Millard are both dead. Wilbur and Elmo are still around, and when we're up to it, we totter over to the truck stop café (the store is long gone, but the new post office was built on the site) and talk about the "good old days."

The only reason to wish those days back would be to have Preacher and Sara among us, but that don't seem fair—the rest of the world needs to experience what it's like having a disaster-producing machine living on the premises. It's a machine that's never worn out, even after all these years.

The Marshalls finally made it to Lima, Peru, and grew as close to the people there as they were here. They outlasted several coups—none of which was blamed on Preacher—and an earthquake or two. A daughter was born there, then a son; they sent me snapshots of the family each year in a Christmas card, which usually got here about the middle of January. Little Amy was the spitting image of Sara, and Michael a chip off the old Preacher block, complete with roostertail hair.

This January came and went and I didn't get a card. I thought they'd given up on me, or else the card got lost in the mail. It never occurred to me that something might have happened to Preacher.

Finally, in yesterday's mail was a long letter from Sister Sara, complete with newspaper clippings. I had forgotten that it's summer in South America when it's winter here, and in December, Preacher and Sara left the kids with friends and took a vacation to see the high mountain city of Cuzco and the ruins of Machu Picchu. Preacher had chartered a light tour plane so they could get a close look at the ancient stone walls.

According to the newspaper article, they must have run into some dense clouds (or maybe Preacher wheedled the pilot into flying lower so they could see better). Anyway, they got a real close look—the plane crash-landed on one of the mountain rock terraces. The newspaper picture showed the crumpled-up little Beechcraft shoved up next to the base of a huge stone altar, which had gotten knocked over and broke.

The miracle was, no one was seriously hurt, except for the altar, which had lasted a thousand years until Preacher Gene Marshall got within range of it. While they waited for help to arrive, Preacher converted the pilot and had some Japanese tourists, who had also been aboard, singing "Trust and Obey" in a mixture of English, Japanese, and Spanish.

She closed the letter saying that after that close call, she and Gene wanted to come see her parents while they were still living—the parents, I mean (although it could have applied just as well to Preacher and Sara). So they applied for a furlough, and they'll be in Texarkana around the first of June to stay for a month. At some point, Sara wrote, they want to drive up to Blacksburg for a visit.

Well, as usual, Preacher's timing's a little off—I'm not quite ready for my funeral. But maybe he can preach a Sunday night mission sermon while he's here. Just wait until he finds out that Loren and Zane McAnelly are deacons.

ABOUT THE AUTHOR

GERALD EUGENE NATHAN STONE was born in 1929 in the South Canadian River bottoms of Oklahoma, near what is now the upstream end of Lake Eufaula. He grew up in Oklahoma and Arkansas, and was graduated from the University of Arkansas with degrees in fine arts (1952) and architecture (1962), with a degree in divinity from Southwestern Baptist Theological Seminary in Fort Worth, Texas, sandwiched between. He now resides with his wife, Virginia, in Denton, Texas, where they reared their four children, and where he has been a principal in The Architectural Collective, Inc. since 1967.